A COZY CHRISTMAS ESCAPE

SNOWY PINE RIDGE BOOK FIVE

FIONA BAKER

Copyright © 2023 by Fiona Baker

All rights reserved. This book or any portion thereof may not be reproduced or used in any manner whatsoever without the express written permission of the publisher except for the use of brief quotations in a book review.

Published in the United States of America

First Edition, 2023

fionabakerauthor.com

JOIN MY NEWSLETTER

If you love beachy, feel-good women's fiction, sign up to receive my newsletter, where you'll get free books, exclusive bonus content, and info on my new releases and sales!

CHAPTER ONE

Valerie Bernard huffed out a breath as she pulled her navy-blue hat down farther across her brow, pushing her bangs into her eyes. She didn't dare brush the hair away though. The long layers of the rest of her shiny, chestnut brown hair stuck out from underneath the cap, cascading down over her shoulders and hiding her face behind a curtain every time she moved.

Or at least, that was what she hoped.

The buzz of the people at LAX surrounded her, washing over her senses like the white noise sounds she so often played from a Bluetooth speaker at night. The background noise of people deep in conversation, the hum of luggage wheels across the linoleum as someone raced from one terminal to the other, the garbled voice coming over the loudspeaker announcing boarding—it all drifted around her to form a cocoon of noise and distraction, and Valerie was delighted when she found that not a single soul had so much as glanced her way.

"Good," she breathed to herself, finally raising her chin to look through the crowd, her gaze flitting over the people gathered around each gate that she passed.

When she made it to her gate, she shifted on her feet nervously before walking toward the corner of the space and taking a seat. It had been a long time since she had flown economy. Over the years, she had grown accustomed to the first-class lounge, but now she tried to remain as inconspicuous as possible as she sank into her seat in the corner, staring out the window that overlooked the tarmac.

"Excuse me," said a quiet, hesitant voice behind her.

Valerie's gaze flicked toward the voice, taking in the blonde-haired young woman standing only a few feet away. Her face was pink cheeked and still maintained some of the roundness of youth, and her blue eyes shone with excited curiosity. Valerie guessed that the girl couldn't be any older than nineteen.

Knowing what was to come, Valerie steeled herself internally and plastered an award-winning smile across her face. It was the same one she had donned a thousand times, whether it was on red carpets, before the camera for a magazine spread, or during moments just like this. Moments when someone recognized her, and she had to turn it on. That thing, that... *it* factor. The one that made her *the* Valerie Bernard.

"I'm so sorry to bother you," the girl continued when she realized she had Valerie's attention. She cleared her throat, seeming a bit nervous. Something about her expression was so endearing that Valerie found herself warming to the girl immediately, and her smile turned genuine.

"Are you... are you Valerie Bernard?" The girl's eyes widened as she whispered the name, as if she was terrified that someone would overhear her and steal Valerie's focus away.

"I am," Valerie answered with a small nod of her head, her grin widening. "And what's your name?"

The girl before her flushed brightly at the question, and her blue eyes sparkled with pure elation. A smile, wide and beaming, spread across the girl's face before she began speaking.

I'm going to miss this, Valerie thought to herself.

This was always the best part. These little moments of connection with strangers.

"My name is Rachel," the girl blurted. "And I'm a huge fan. *The Edge of You* is one of my favorite movies of all time. I think I've watched it at least a hundred times."

Valerie laughed, a deep, throaty sound that entertainment journalists liked to make fun of, saying that she was trying too hard. They never took into account the fact that Valerie's voice had a natural rasp, and that she had laughed like that for her entire life.

"It was one of my favorites to star in," she answered honestly, thinking back to the friends she had made on that particular film set. Many of her co-stars were people she was still friends with.

"I know you're at the airport," Rachel continued in a rush. "And you're probably, like, waiting to board the plane to go off and do something really cool and just want time to rest. But would it be too much to ask to get a picture with you?"

"We can absolutely take a picture." Valerie grinned.

It took Rachel a second to get the phone out of her pocket, and once she did, it took her another moment to pull up her camera app. The poor girl was so nervous that she was shaking, and Valerie did her best to hide the amusement that threatened to break out across her features.

"Okay, I've got it," Rachel finally announced as she held her phone up in the air.

She turned her back to Valerie, holding the device up high to get her in the shot from a distance, and Valerie couldn't help but laugh.

"You can come closer," Valerie said, patting the hard plastic seat next to her. "I don't mind."

She didn't know how it was possible, but Rachel's cheeks flushed an even deeper shade of crimson. The smile and the joy never once fell from the girl's face as she took a few steps to close the distance between them. Rachel took a seat on the chair beside Valerie, perching on the edge of it like she was terrified of disturbing the actress, despite the fact that it was Valerie herself who had advised the girl to sit there in the first place.

"Scoot in." Valerie waved her hands, motioning for Rachel to get closer.

The girl did as she was told, beaming through her disbelief as Valerie encouraged her to crowd into the frame of the camera with her. They pressed their faces close together, almost cheek to cheek as they both grinned widely, and Rachel snapped several selfies of the two of them.

"This is perfect!" Rachel exclaimed as she looked at the pictures. "Thank you so much!"

"It was my pleasure," Valerie answered genuinely.

"Are you starring in anything soon?" Rachel asked, looking eager.

Valerie tried to keep her smile from faltering, to keep the muscle in her jaw from twitching, as the girl's question hit her like a ton of bricks.

But Rachel must have noticed the shift in Valerie, because she shook her head quickly as she said, "I'm sorry. I didn't mean to pry. I should probably get going or I'll miss my flight."

The girl stood up, but before she strode away, she looked back down at Valerie.

"But seriously, Ms. Bernard…"

"Valerie, please," Valerie corrected gently.

"Valerie." Rachel tried again, color still high in her cheeks. "Thank you for being so kind and for taking a picture with me. I promise, I'll scream from the rooftops that you're the nicest celebrity I've ever met."

"Have you met many?" Valerie asked with a chuckle, and Rachel shook her head.

"Well... no. Just you," she answered, her nerves seeming to fade a little as they shared a laugh. "But thank you again."

Valerie nodded at the girl, still smiling as she watched Rachel's blonde head disappear through the crowd, rushing off toward her gate. A few people had turned their attention to her, likely seeing the interaction between her and Rachel, and Valerie shrank back into her seat.

She tugged the brim of her hat farther down, disguising her face as much as she could. She might have loved meeting Rachel, but the last thing she wanted was for an actual fuss to be made over her being there. Luckily, just as she saw one other woman seem to be plucking up the courage to come talk to her, the announcements for boarding started, and people became distracted once more.

Valerie was so used to boarding with first class that when they called for it that she almost got up to join that line. But she stopped herself just in time, staying seated as the first-class passengers boarded.

It wasn't that she couldn't afford to fly first class any longer. Throughout her years in the limelight, she had made plenty of money, and she had a nest egg that she could easily survive off of for the rest of her life. But Valerie had figured that people were more likely to recognize her if she flew first class. She supposed people typically didn't expect movie stars, especially ones who were just barely out of their prime, to be flying coach. So maybe if someone recognized her, they would second-guess themselves when they realized that she was sitting in the very back of the plane.

It wasn't a foolproof plan, but it was all she had.

When the call was finally made for her economy group to begin boarding, Valerie rose to her feet and tucked her Kindle into her oversized purse. She had checked her two other suitcases, and she was glad that she didn't have to worry about them as she walked through the waiting area toward the line that was forming in front of the attendant at the gate.

As she slowly made her way through the line and then onto the boarding bridge, Valerie's mind began to wander. She tried to steer her thoughts clear of her career, but no matter what she did, her mind kept drifting back to her meeting with Rachel and the question the girl had asked right before she'd left.

Are you starring in anything soon?

Rachel had seemed so eager and excited when she'd asked, as if she just knew the answer was going to be something outrageous and fantastic. She had probably already been thinking about what quippy caption she would write when she published their selfies on Instagram.

Valerie could all but see it in her mind's eye.

I can't believe who I met at the airport today! Rachel might write. *She was so nice, and be sure to check out her new movie soon! Valerie Bernard says it's going to be a box office smash!*

Only... there was no movie. There would be no box office smash. There was nothing for Valerie anymore when it came to acting. Or at least, that was what it felt like.

Valerie let out a long, quiet sigh as she finally boarded the plane. Her bag jostled against the closely packed seats as she walked between them, looking for row K. She had at least gotten a window seat, and she was grateful when she found the row empty and was able to slide right across to it. Valerie gazed out the window, watching the airport workers wave neon sticks and drive carts filled with luggage as the other passengers filed onto the plane.

But still, nothing could keep her thoughts away from the disaster that had become her acting career.

She had been in the business for a very long time, having starred in a few short films, commercials, and plays while growing up. It had never been anything big back then. Her mother had been too insistent that she have a normal childhood in Montana, refusing to allow her to work enough to ever be considered a 'child star.' But it was certainly enough for Valerie to fall in love with acting.

She'd moved from Montana to Los Angeles almost the very same day she had turned eighteen. After arriving in the entertainment capital of the country, she had bussed tables, made lattes, and worked as a server to pay for the small studio apartment that she'd shared with two other girls in West Hollywood just to get by.

The day that Grace Maloney, one of the biggest names in movies at that time, had strode into the restaurant Valerie had been working at, Valerie had known that luck was on her side. She had delved into her bag and grabbed one of her audition tapes, something that she'd happened to have on her in order to submit herself for a supporting role in a low-budget indie film.

By giving the tape to Grace, she'd known that she would be losing out on her chance for the other movie, but she'd also known that another opportunity like the one before her wouldn't happen again any time soon.

So she had risked it.

Grace had been kind and taken the tape. And

when she had left by the end of the night, she had promised to watch it and pass it along to her agent. Still, Valerie had doubted anything would come of it. So when a call had come from Grace's agent the very next day telling her that she had incredible talent and he wanted to sign her, Valerie had been floored.

At nineteen, Valerie had been hired for her first role in a major film. A speaking role. A *named character*. It wasn't huge, just the main character's plucky best friend who helped her heal her heartbreak and provided much needed comic relief. But it had been enough. Enough to get her in front of the A-List cast and crew. And enough to launch her into stardom very shortly afterward.

She had worked steadily for nearly ten years. But as Valerie's thirtieth birthday had drawn closer, the conversations surrounding her had begun to shift.

People no longer cared about what she wore on the red carpet, or who she had been caught talking to at an awards party. No, what they cared about now was the fact that she had decided to do something as wild and unheard of as not getting Botox and now had a single, solitary wrinkle by the corner of her mouth. What they cared about wasn't *who* she was dating, but the fact that she wasn't dating at all. That she was approaching thirty and she had no husband and no children.

Over the years, she had gotten used to the media picking apart her appearance, but the vitriol with which they came at her as she approached and then turned thirty had been something else entirely. And when the desirable roles had ultimately dried up, leaving behind only the ones like 'Frumpy Mom in a Teenage Sitcom,' Valerie had allowed herself to panic.

She had locked herself in her Beverly Hills home and drunk more bottles of wine from her coveted collection than she cared to admit while watching old Marilyn Monroe films. Valerie had ordered takeout for every meal and had worn a particularly nostalgic pair of sweats for three days straight before she finally convinced herself to take a shower.

It was right after that particular shower, with her hair still sopping wet but wearing a new pair of soft—and more importantly, clean—sweatpants that she had seen it. It was on the back of a magazine, one that had fallen face down on her coffee table after she had gotten frustrated while reading yet another gossip column asking 'What's Going on With Valerie Bernard?."

THE EAST COAST'S BEST KEPT SECRET,

the ad read in bold blue letters at the top of the page. The words were superimposed over the image of a woman and a man smiling lovingly at a child who was attempting to ski down a bunny hill. A mountain range loomed in the distance, snow-capped peaks glistening in the sun. And at the bottom of the page, a familiar name was scrawled in the same blue font. SNOWY PINE RIDGE.

The name had jostled something in her memory, something about a place that her mother had gone to years and years ago, before Valerie had even been born. But the place had had such a profound impact on Valerie's mother that decades later, she had still referred to it as being filled with magic.

And right now, Valerie could use some of that magic.

Plus, since she very publicly disliked skiing—or any outdoor activity, really—she knew that absolutely no one would ever think to look for her in a town like that. Which made Snowy Pine Ridge an absolutely perfect destination for her to run away to so that she could clear her head.

Something bumped against Valerie's leg, ripping her focus away from her past and planting her firmly back in the present. She glanced over at the sweaty man who was sitting in the middle seat, his legs splayed much farther apart than they needed to be, and then at the woman who sat on the other side of him.

She and the woman locked eyes, then both of them shook their heads as they settled back into their seats, neither of them thinking it was worth the fight.

The plane began to rumble, and the voice of the pilot sounded over the speakers as a flight attendant appeared at the very front of the plane. The safety instructions began as the vessel started to move across the tarmac, and Valerie took that as her cue to extract her neck pillow and sleeping mask from the large purse on the floor between her feet.

With the pillow and the mask firmly in place, she ignored her overbearing seat mate and decided to focus on the positives. Soon she would be on the opposite side of the country, in a town covered in snow and, if her mother had been right, filled with magic. She would be spending the holidays in a place where she could relax. Where she could hopefully find herself again—or at the very least, get a bit of clarity.

Snowy Pine Ridge, here I come, she thought.

CHAPTER TWO

Fat, fluffy flecks of snow flitted by the window as Clark Mitchell flipped the page on the inventory magazine he'd been perusing. The hardware store was silent, not a single soul inside the place except for him, and when he glanced at the clock he knew why. It was nearly six o'clock in the evening, only about an hour before it would be time to close.

A winter storm had also blown through Snowy Pine Ridge two days before, and it had been a real doozy. The roads had only just become drivable early that afternoon, with the plows working overtime for two days straight just to keep up with the amount of snow that had continued to fall.

Thankfully, it had begun to slow down a bit recently, and the snowflakes that currently fell from the sky were sporadic. It wasn't anything that would accumulate further.

Just as Clark was thinking he might close up the shop early, since no one was likely to venture into the store at this hour, a figure materialized in the small pool of light outside cast by the windows and the fluorescents of Mitchell's Hardware.

Clark squinted as the figure approached. Whoever it was, they were entirely concealed in a dark coat with the hood pulled up around their face. It wasn't until the person pulled open the door, stepped inside, and began to speak that Clark recognized the man as his friend, Derek Morse.

"I know you're likely getting ready to close up shop," Derek said. "But is it alright if I come in for a few things?"

"Of course," Clark answered, watching as Derek kicked the snow from his boots and pushed down his hood. "We've still got another hour before I officially close. So take your time."

Derek nodded, uncharacteristically quiet as he walked farther into the store. As he got closer, Clark was able to get a better look at his friend, and he couldn't help but notice the dark circles under Derek's eyes and the exhaustion that seemed to hunch his shoulders.

"Everything going alright?" Clark asked as Derek grabbed a shopping basket and began walking through the well-stocked shelves.

Derek ran a gloved hand through his auburn hair, causing it to become damp with snow. Clark thought for a moment to warn him to stop, that the damp hair would make him sick if he went outside with it like that. But then he realized that lecturing his friend like that would only serve to make him sound like his grandmother, and Derek would never let him hear the end of it.

"Yeah, things are fine. I'm just tired," Derek answered as he disappeared from Clark's line of sight. "Piper has a cold, and she hasn't slept much since before the storm. Which means neither have Lacy or I."

Piper was Derek and Lacy's nearly one-year-old daughter. Despite being so small, generally sweet tempered, and absurdly adorable, the baby girl had a wild streak large enough to rival her father's when he'd been growing up. So Clark could only imagine what the child was like when she wasn't feeling well.

"Anything in particular you're looking for?" Clark asked, his brow furrowing as he walked out from behind the counter toward where Derek was standing.

"I got some blackout curtains," his friend explained as he eyed the shelves. "Maybe those will help her sleep. Do you have the stuff to hang something like that?"

Clark nodded and began leading Derek through the small store. Clark had grown up in Mitchell's Hardware, and the shop had been passed down through generations of family members before being left in his care. He had made a few improvements over the years, expanding some of the inventory as the needs of the town had begun to change. But much of it remained the same as it had been on the day it had been founded by his great-great grandfather. And as such, he knew the store like the back of his hand.

It didn't take him long to fill Derek's basket with all of the supplies that he needed, his friend chatting his ear off about his baby and his wife all the while. Clark was glad to hear about them, since he'd become good friends with Lacy in the time since she'd moved to Snowy Pine Ridge as well.

But listening to Derek talk about his family also filled Clark with a strange pulling sensation deep within his belly—an untold yearning for something that everyone else seemed to have, but which he himself did not. A family of his own.

At thirty-three, Clark couldn't help but feel as if life was in the midst of leaving him behind. Sure, he was a successful business owner, and he had an amazing group of friends. But outside of that?

His friends and their wives always told him that he was a catch. But if that were true, why did he seem to have so much trouble making anything that even resembled romance stick? Looking at Derek, Clark could see it in his eyes. Despite the exhaustion and stress of dealing with a sick baby, his friend was clearly deeply in love with his wife, his child, and his life. And Clark couldn't help but be a little bit jealous, even as he felt happy for Derek.

The two men walked back to the checkout counter, and Clark began to ring up the items Derek had selected. He pushed his thoughts of family and that small twinge of jealousy out of his mind as he and his friend continued to talk. But it didn't take long before they were interrupted by a blast of cold air when the door was pried open once more.

"Wow. Apparently, the hardware store is the place to be this evening," Clark joked as Matthew Martinez, the local real estate agent, strode through the door.

Matthew was wearing his usual camel colored Carhartt jacket, with no other protection from the cold, and his blue eyes immediately fell on the two men standing in the shop. His face lit with a grin as he took in Derek and Clark, and he kicked the snow from his boots off before closing the distance between them.

"This is perfect," Matthew said, his warm voice filling the space. "After I was done chatting with Clark, I was going to come see you, Derek. So this will save me a trip!"

Derek took out his wallet, sliding his card into the card reader as Clark told him his total, then both of them fixed the newcomer with twin looks of curiosity.

"What's going on?" Clark asked.

"You know the storm that blew through here a couple of days ago?" Matthew began, and both Clark and Derek nodded, confirming that they knew exactly what he was talking about. "It did some major damage to the Hilton family's house. The whole roof caved in."

Clark's eyebrows shot up in shock as Derek made a low noise of surprise.

"Are they all right?" Derek asked.

"Thankfully, yes." Matthew nodded, his sandy brown hair glinting beneath the overhead light. "But their house isn't, obviously. The good news is, I have a house that was in foreclosure that I'm going to get them set up in. Only thing is, it isn't livable just yet."

Matthew was the premiere real estate agent in the area. Almost every single house that was sold or apartment that was rented went through him. He also handled more delicate matters, such as foreclosures, and could often be found doing charity work or building houses for the needy outside of Snowy Pine Ridge. So the fact that he had decided to fix up a space for a family in need was no surprise at all to Clark.

"So," Matthew prompted, looking hopeful. "What do you say? Would you two be able to help out with getting the house ready for occupants?"

"Absolutely," Clark answered, not needing even a moment to think about it.

Derek's response was almost as fast as Clark's. "Of course. Whatever you need."

Matthew smiled at the two of them. "I knew I could count on you. Thank you so much! With any luck, we can get them into their new place in time for Christmas so that their holiday won't be completely ruined."

They began going over the details, with Clark offering to cover whatever materials he could, as well as providing his services as a handyman. Having a basic knowledge of carpentry, home renovation, and power tools sort of came with the territory of owning a hardware store, and Clark had made it a point to learn as much as he could about his trade. So fixing up a house was right up his alley.

Derek agreed that he could help with some of the heavy lifting, as well as provide two trucks to help transport the materials that would be needed. Derek and Lacy owned Winter Run Racing, a dogsled business that offered rides, provided training, and was also a retailer. The constant hauling of supplies and of dogs meant that he had two large trucks that belonged to the business. Both of which Derek advised Matthew were now at his disposal.

"That's fantastic. Thank you!" Matthew beamed as they ironed out a few more details, agreeing to get started the very next day.

The three men said their goodbyes, and when both Derek and Matthew had disappeared out the door, the snow and the winter night swallowing them up, Clark blew out a breath. It wasn't exactly seven yet, not quite closing time, but he flipped the sign on the door from OPEN to CLOSED anyway.

It had been a long day—not a bad one, just a long one—and Clark was more than ready to make his way home and have a hearty meal before heading to bed. After closing down the shop and turning off the lights, he grabbed his coat, shrugging it on before he walked out the door.

He stopped only long enough to lock up behind himself before he strode down the sidewalk, surrounded by the glow of Christmas lights from the nearby businesses.

CHAPTER THREE

"The kids are late," Rudolph Hutchins grumbled as he walked past Shelley Keegan, prompting her to glance down at her watch.

"Oh no, they are not," she said with a chuckle, shaking her head slightly at the grumpy man before her.

She was standing by the doors of the Happy Glacier Ice Rink, the skating rink that Rudolph owned. Although Shelley had once struggled with her past failures as Olympic-level figure skater, she had rediscovered her love of the ice after coming to Snowy Pine Ridge, and she'd ended up becoming a skating teacher at the rink. Despite Rudolph's gruff complaints, her latest batch of students still had nearly ten minutes before they were even supposed to be there.

"Didn't anyone ever teach them that if they arrive on time, then they're considered late?" Rudolph grumbled, narrowing his eyes as he came to stand beside Shelley and glower out at the parking lot.

"Is that what *you* were taught?" she asked, trying and failing to hide the amusement in her voice.

"Sure was." The man next to her harrumphed just as a minivan pulled into the parking lot.

"See?" Shelley pointed toward it. "Looks like they're early."

"On time is more like it," the old man muttered, turning away and walking toward the counter where the kids would collect their skates.

Shelley watched him with a smile as a few kids piled out of the minivan and another SUV pulled in beside it. When she had come to Snowy Pine Ridge a couple of years ago, she had been fleeing her old life—or what she had originally envisioned her life to be, anyway.

Ever since she'd been young, the only thing she had wanted to be was an Olympic figure skater. But those dreams had been shattered when she had suffered a career-ending injury thanks to a painful and humiliating fall during a routine. After that, she had fled to this town to try to figure out some way to cope with the loss of her dream.

But what she had found here had turned out to be better than anything she could've ever imagined for herself. Because not only had Snowy Pine Ridge become her home, but it had led her to the love of her life, Matthew, and his son that she had also come to love like her own. This snowy little town had given her a home and a family. And eventually, it had also given her these classes, where she could teach children how to ice skate and pass on some of her knowledge to them. In doing so, it had reignited the passion within her. A passion that she thought had gone dormant along with her Olympic career.

As the kids began pouring out of their parents' vehicles and traipsing across the parking lot, Shelley threw a quick look over her shoulder toward the owner of the rink. Rudolph was on the other side of the building, behind the counter typically used for ice skate rental. She watched as he picked out the sizes he knew that they'd need for the kids that didn't yet have their own skates, picking out the best ones that he could while muttering to himself about the inconvenience of it all. But despite his words and his blatant complaints, he couldn't quite hide the joy that was dancing behind his eyes. Which only served to convince Shelley that his current grumpiness was nothing more than an act.

Rudolph was well known around town for being a bit of a curmudgeon. His usual stodgy demeanor was something almost every single person in Snowy Pine Ridge was familiar with. But ever since Shelley had launched her classes, she had begun to see a different side of the man.

He was still grumpy and still complained about every single thing that occurred around the rink. But it didn't have the same level of gusto as his complaints about the other goings-on around town. More than once, Shelley had caught him watching the children as they skated, nailing tricks and choreography that they had only dreamed of doing when they first began, and smiling.

Of course, the moment that he had noticed Shelley watching, he'd immediately reaffixed his usual scowl on his face and walked off muttering to himself. But it didn't change the fact that she had caught him in the first place. Not that Rudolph would ever admit to it, but Shelley had long since figured out that the old man was not only tolerating these classes but was actually enjoying them.

Sound rushed through the roller rink as the door

was pulled open, and boys and girls began sprinting through the space. They ran by Shelley, yelling greetings at her as they made their way to Rudolph and the benches by the counter so they could begin putting on their skates. The moment they reached the area where the old man stood, his face broke out in a grin as he began talking to them, handing over the skates to the ones that needed them. And before long, she was out on the ice with all of them, beginning her instruction and leaving Rudolph to his own devices.

She glanced in his direction a few times, noticing that while he was technically working, he never strayed far from the area of the ice rink. And as the training time began to dwindle and the final ten minutes approached, an idea struck her.

"All right," Shelley called out, and the wide-eyed gazes of all the children alighted on her. "We're down to the last ten minutes. You all know what that means!"

"Free skate!" The kids all yelled in unison before they started to skate around at random, trying to work on whatever their hearts desired as the time for their parents to pick them up approached.

Shelley usually stayed out on the ice with them, but this time around she turned her back toward them and made her way off the rink to where Rudolph was standing, watching through the glass.

"I need to run to the restroom and grab some water," she fibbed effortlessly. "Do you want to take over and watch them for a little bit?"

"You want me to watch the little buggers?" Rudolph asked, affixing a scowl to his face despite the sparkle in his eyes at the thought.

"I'll be back so fast you don't even realize I'm gone," Shelley explained, kicking off her skates before he could protest and scurried toward the hallway that led to the bathroom.

The moment that Shelley knew she was out of sight, she pressed herself back against the wall as she waited for a minute or two to pass. When she felt like it had been long enough that Rudolph would have turned his attention back toward the children, she peeked her head out from the hallway to see what he was doing.

Her mouth popped open in a small 'o' of surprise when she saw him sitting at one of the benches, lacing up a pair of his own skates as a few of the children cheered him on. He skated onto the ice with them without so much as looking back in her direction, launching into a race between a couple of the kids and him.

No longer caring if the old man saw her, she stepped out of the hallway and stood, leaning against the wall as she watched Rudolph come to life as he skated around the rink with the kids. By the time the front doors were pulled open and the first of the parents arrived, the owner of the rink was red-faced and laughing.

"Is that Rudolph?" a voice said beside her, and she glanced to the side to find Pamela Murphy, a mother of one of the kids, staring with wide-eyed shock at the ice rink.

"It sure is," Shelley said with a smile, warmth spreading through her as she turned her attention back toward the ice.

She found it hard to believe just how much Rudolph seemed to come alive during these moments with the kids. And if the murmuring from the parents who had just walked in the door was any indicator, they felt exactly the same way.

The large digital clock at the far end of the wall let out a loud, bleating trill, announcing the time and the kids all groaned before turning to double check that their parents were there. Rudolph, who apparently had lost all track of time, blinked his eyes rapidly and his head swiveled to the newly gathered crowd. He balked when he saw all the other townsfolk watching him, murmuring to themselves about the rarity of finding Rudolph Hutchins having fun. And then he skated off the ice as quickly as he could, disappearing behind the counter once more to help the kids return their skates.

Shelley laughed and shook her head, turning her attention back to the parents and the children that were lining up to leave. She was swept away in a flurry of goodbyes and 'see you next weeks', and it felt like the next thing she knew, she had blinked, and the children were making their way back across the parking lot toward their parents' vehicles.

The rink was silent again, so silent that Shelley felt a slight ringing in her ears as she walked toward where Rudolph was disinfecting the used skates.

"You seemed like you had quite a bit of fun tonight," she quipped, reaching up to tuck a strand of short blonde hair back into the ponytail at the nape of her neck. "I haven't seen you smile like that in... well... ever."

Rudolph's dark brown eyes flicked up to hers, scowl still firmly in place.

"They bet me that I couldn't beat them in a race around the rink," he huffed.

"And did you beat them?" Shelley arched an

eyebrow at him, despite the fact that she already knew the answer.

One corner of his mouth tugged up in a smug smile. "'Course I did."

Shelley laughed. "You looked like you know your way around a rink. That's for sure. That's the first time I've ever seen you skate."

His brow furrowed and he regarded her skeptically. "Is there a question there?"

Shelley shook her head. "No. Just making conversation. I figured you could skate, since you own an ice rink and everything. I've just never seen you do it before."

"I like to skate."

His words were blunt and bit off at the end, clearly indicating that he didn't want to talk about it anymore. And something about the way that he seemed so incredibly reluctant to talk about it at all, made Shelley pretty sure that there was a lot more to the story than Rudolph was letting on.

But since this was the most she had ever heard the man speak in her entire time in Snowy Pine Ridge, she wasn't going to press the issue and have him clam up all over again. She reached forward and plucked a pair of skates off the counter, grabbing the disinfectant and began to help him.

"So are you excited about the 12 Days of Christmas showcase coming up? Feeling prepared?" she asked curiously.

In a few weeks, the town was hosting a holiday celebration, aptly named the 12 Days of Christmas Showcase. One group of kids that she was currently working with was going to be putting on a performance during it, and the preparations were well under way.

"Don't know if excited is the right word," Rudolph grunted, but his words held no bite. "I'm ready though. Got a whole light show planned for the little buggers."

Her eyebrows shot up. "For the kids' show?"

He nodded, seemingly unable to stop the proud grin that spread across his lips. "Yup. It's really going to be something."

"Tell me more. Will we need to switch around the choreography or anything?"

He shook his head. "Nothing like that."

And then he launched into a grand explanation of what he had envisioned and how he pictured it all coming together in his mind. The more he talked, the more his air of grumpiness fell to the wayside. He described in great detail the way the lights would wrap around the rink and how they would light up in time to the kids' movements, his hands gesticulating wildly as he spoke. And by the end of his spiel, she could see it all in her mind's eye too.

"That's going to be absolutely amazing, Rudolph." She grinned at him as they finished up the final pairs of skates and placed them on the shelving unit behind them. "Everyone is going to love it."

"Yeah, well." He shrugged one shoulder, turning to face her now that the job was complete. "Can't have you making a fool of me and my rink."

"Wouldn't dream of it," she joked.

Shelley couldn't be entirely sure, but she was almost certain that the corner of Rudolph's mouth ticked up in an amused smile.

* * *

Valerie grunted with effort as she lifted her suitcase and plopped it onto the bed before opening it. Her belongings all came spilling out of it the moment the pressure from the zipper was released. She had sized down from the amount of stuff she usually brought while traveling, not wanting to draw attention to herself at baggage claim and while navigating the airport. And the nondescript black bag that she had bought specifically for the occasion barely held half of what she was used to.

She stopped for a second, blowing back a piece of chestnut hair that had fallen down into her face from the ponytail she'd pulled her hair into, and eyed some of the contents now spread across the duvet. She had most of the necessities, but there were a few things she'd have to run out and buy. Namely- candles. She found something so cozy about the act of lighting candles and loving having them burning while she relaxed with a book. Tearing her attention away from her things, Valerie placed her hands on her hips, spinning in place to take in the room that she'd been given.

The Warm and Bright Hotel was definitely charming, she'd give it that. Her room was filled with blush pink and pastels, and small, silver and pink Christmas ornaments dangling from the curtains, as well as the petite white Christmas tree that was in the corner. In the center of the room was a massive, four poster bed that she couldn't help but immediately want to collapse into, and on the other side of the room was a large wooden armoire for her to place her clothes.

Valerie walked through the room, trailing her fingers over the soft fabrics as she went before flicking on the light to the attached bathroom. The floor was black and white tile, complementing the blush pink and silver accents throughout the rest of the space. A clawfoot tub was in one corner, as well as a walk-in shower on the other side of the room. She had no idea who had been in charge of decorating her room in particular, but whoever they were, Valerie had to give them credit. They had an incredible eye for combining both modern and traditional designs while still making it feel so incredibly cozy and festive for the holiday season.

She threw another glance over her shoulder, glaring at the suitcase still open on the bed. It was like it was taunting her, telling her that if she didn't unpack it now, she would regret it later, but she was also exhausted after her day of travel.

"I'll deal with you later," she said to the luggage, deliberately ignoring the fact that she was now talking to inanimate objects.

She walked out of the room and through the beautifully decorated hallway. The light wooden floors were polished and gleaming, with a red, ornate runner marking her path. She followed it gladly, her brown eyes raking over the pictures that adorned the walls as she went.

Painted canvases were mixed in with

photographs, each one showing something different around town. Some of them were clearly recent, while others had the sepia tone and clearly frayed edges that betrayed their age. Each one told the story of the town as it grew and changed over the years, showing an array of smiling faces and beautiful, technicolor lives.

By the time she reached the first floor of the building, the smell of apple muffins and warmed apple cider floated out from the dining room to greet her. She sniffed the air delicately, following the smell until she found the goods laid out on a serving table. There was a small, hand carved sign in front of the platters that read *'help yourself'* and Valerie smiled.

"Don't mind if I do," she whispered as she picked up one of the small white plates next to the offerings.

She looked a little more closely at the design before she chose a muffin, noting the small motif of mistletoe directly in the center of the plate. Valerie had always loved attention to detail, and so far, it appeared that the Warm and Bright Hotel had it in droves.

She turned her attention back to the platters laid out on the table, and carefully selected a muffin that appeared to have the perfect amount of crispy apple crumble on top and plopped it onto the plate. Just as she began to fill up one of the mugs on the table from the large thermos of hot cider, a voice sounded from behind her.

"Are you enjoying everything so far, dear?"

A squeak of surprise flew past Valerie's lips and her heart pounded wildly. She whirled toward the voice, finding herself staring at a stylish woman who, Valerie guessed, was likely in her late sixties. The woman had white hair that was elegantly twisted away from her face into a chignon, a bright red cashmere sweater, and black, beautifully tailored trousers. A string of pearls wound its way around her throat, and her blue eyes sparkled as she looked at Valerie with a warm, amused smile.

"I'm so sorry," the older woman said with a low chuckle. "I didn't mean to startle you. I thought you heard me approach."

Valerie's hand had fluttered to her chest, hovering right above her heart, whose rhythm was finally beginning to return to normal.

"I didn't," she responded with a shaky laugh.

She looked down at the mug in her hand, thankful that she hadn't actually put any of the cider in it yet. If she had, she was sure that it would have gone flying as she jumped when the woman startled her.

"My name is Evelyn." The woman extended an elegant hand toward Valerie. "The owner of the Warm and Bright Hotel."

Valerie took her hand and gave it a quick shake.

"Valerie," she said, offering her first name only and hoping that the hotel proprietor didn't watch too many movies.

"Oh, don't worry, love," Evelyn quipped, her blue eyes twinkling. "I know exactly who you are. I recognized your name the moment I saw it in our reservation books."

Valerie's stomach did a somersault. She suddenly wondered if coming to Snowy Pine Ridge had been the right call after all. Her face must have betrayed the sudden turn of her feelings, because Evelyn's silver brows suddenly creased with concern.

"I hope that didn't come out wrong," Evelyn began to explain. "Believe me. I love your movies, but I don't put much stock into fame or celebrity. So, while I'm a fan of your work, I see it as just that. Work. Just like what I do here."

She gestured wide, encompassing the beautiful building they were standing in. Valerie gave herself a second to study the woman's face, wondering if maybe she was only laying it on a little thick because having a celebrity stay at her hotel would be good for business, but she didn't catch any hint of deception from Evelyn. Quite the opposite, actually.

Evelyn seemed to exude a sense of well put together welcome. Every bit of her was perfectly coiffed and curated, but somehow none of it seemed fake. She just *was*. And with that in mind, Valerie didn't find it hard to believe that someone who carried themselves in that manner wouldn't buy into the glory of fame.

She smiled then, a genuine one, and the little bit of tension that had made its way into Evelyn's forehead relaxed.

"I know I interrupted you getting some cider," Evelyn said, stepping forward and grabbing a mug of her own. "Please, continue."

She waved a hand toward the thermos that Valerie was standing in front of, and Valerie turned, going back to filling her mug.

"You know," Evelyn said, stepping up to fill her own cup once Valerie was finished. "I find that one of the best ways to unwind after a long day is to sit on the front porch with a mug of hot tea, or..." She raised her now full mug. "Cider. Why don't you join me?"

Valerie considered for a moment, her mind wandering toward the suitcase on her bed that was still crammed full of her belongings. She knew that she should go upstairs and begin organizing everything so that she wouldn't have to do it later. She hated living out of suitcases, and she hated clutter. But the offer that Evelyn had given was so tempting, she couldn't find it within her to say no.

She nodded. "All right."

Evelyn's only answer was a smile before she turned and began to make her way toward the front door, leaving Valerie to trot after her while she tried not to spill her cider. As she walked past one of the tables, her gaze caught on a stack of magazines and her heart began to pound. Her steps faltered for a second, but a quick scan told her that her name wasn't on a single one of them. She let out a quick, relieved breath and followed after Evelyn once more.

When she reached the front door, she found Evelyn pulling a couple of big fleece blankets from a trunk beside it.

"I keep these here in case anyone wants to sit out there while it's cold," she explained. "There's also a small space heater out there for us to place at our feet. It'll keep us nice and toasty."

Evelyn held open the door for Valerie, blankets still draped over her arms and then pointed her toward two rocking chairs about halfway down the wraparound porch. The white-haired woman stood and waited for Valerie to set down the muffin and her mug, before gracefully extending one of her arms to her.

Valerie took the blanket that was draped over it, the cold air already nipping at the tip of her nose and draped it around herself. Immediately the warmth of the blanket enveloped her, and she sighed as she sank back into the chair. Evelyn bent over by her feet, turning on the heater that was sitting there, and angling it so that it would reach toward the back of both of their blankets, blowing warm air into their already cozy cocoons. And in just a few seconds, Valerie hardly even noticed the cold.

She reached next to her, picking up her mug of cider and took a sip, the warmth from the amber liquid chasing away the last bit of chill that was hanging around.

"You're right," Valerie admitted, raising the mug to her lips to take another quick drink. "This is pretty great."

"Saying 'I told you so' is beneath me," Evelyn joked, giving her a wink.

As Valerie chuckled, she found herself beginning to warm up to this woman. They sat in silence for a few moments, giving Valerie time to bite into her muffin. It was as delicious as it looked. The taste of apple, cinnamon, and caramel exploded across her tongue, and she managed to finish the entire pastry in no time at all. Surprisingly enough, the silence between them didn't feel awkward. It was more like the silence that might fall between two people who had known each other for years and were happy simply to bask in each other's presence.

Which was odd, Valerie thought, considering she had only known the woman for all of five minutes. But she decided not to second-guess it. She had come out to Snowy Pine Ridge for a change of pace, after all. And maybe this instant comfort, which was something she always struggled to find when she was in Hollywood, was the universe's way of letting Valerie know that she was on the right track.

"So," Evelyn said, leaning back farther into her chair and beginning to rock herself slightly. "What brought you to Snowy Pine Ridge?"

Valerie considered for a moment, allowing herself the time to decide just how much she wanted to divulge. But the more she thought about it, the more she realized she didn't really want to hide the truth. At least, not right now.

"It all got to be so much," she admitted with a sigh.

"How so?" Evelyn cocked her head, her blue eyes turning pensive as she looked at Valerie.

"When I first started acting," Valerie began. "I loved it. And don't get me wrong, I still do. But everything is so fresh. When you take off the way I did, you're everyone's darling. It was amazing. People couldn't get enough. The tabloids were always talking about me, harmless stuff, usually. Just guessing who I was dating, showing snapshots of me with my morning Starbucks. Interviews that talked about my ambition, and my talent. Little girls asking me for advice, that kind of thing."

Her words died out and a soft pain started in her chest as it occurred to her just how much everything had changed.

"And it's not like that anymore." Evelyn didn't phrase it as a question, but Valerie nodded anyway before continuing.

"The older I got, the more things began to shift. And now, all anyone can talk about is my age. I've decided to allow myself to age gracefully, opting out of Botox and fillers. There's nothing wrong with either of those things as far as I'm concerned. Whatever floats your boat. I just didn't feel like having to keep up with it all. But somehow the media took that as this supreme, giant statement.

"I did *one* interview with *Good Morning America* where I talked about the fact that I was going to let myself grow older. And then all of a sudden it was this giant news story. Everyone either loved it or hated it. But most of them hated it. And then, the media, well, let's just say it all took a turn for the worst. Especially now that they think I've aged out of the business."

Evelyn scoffed. "They think you're old?"

"Yeah." Valerie nodded. "Thirty is ancient as far as L.A. is concerned."

"Honey," Evelyn said. "I'm sixty-seven and I'm not old. So there's no way you're old. You're practically an infant."

Valerie threw her head back and laughed, feeling light despite the heavy content of their conversation.

"You're not wrong," she answered, still chuckling. "But that's why I came out here. When you hit my age in L.A., everyone expects you to go down one very specific path. And I'm just not sure that it's for me."

She shrugged one shoulder and took another sip of her cider.

"Well, for whatever the word of this old crone is worth," Evelyn said, raising one perfectly shaped eyebrow. "They're fools if they're trying to box you in. Whatever it is you decide to do, you're going to be fantastic at it. And if they can't see that, that's on them."

The corner of Valerie's mouth tugged up in a grin. "I thought you weren't old."

Evelyn laughed. "You catch on fast, kid. And I have a feeling you're going to fit right in here in Snowy Pine Ridge."

Valerie's smile grew as she settled down farther in her chair, letting Evelyn's praise wash over her. And as she looked out at the beautiful, snow-covered grounds that surrounded the hotel, she couldn't help the little kernel of hope that began to unfurl in her chest, feeling like Evelyn might be right.

CHAPTER FOUR

Clark swiped his hand across his face, brushing away a dark curl that had fallen onto his forehead as he bent over the dogsled, giving his wrench one final turn.

"I think that's it," he huffed, sitting back on his haunches to study his handiwork.

"Thanks, man," Derek said, ducking his head to look at the repairs that Clark had performed. "It's exactly what it needed."

Derek had shown up at the hardware store about an hour before, standing on the back of a sled being pulled by a team of yapping, excited huskies. Which, surprisingly enough, was not an uncommon event in Snowy Pine Ridge. One of the boards of the sled had worked its way loose while he had been out doing training exercises, and he'd swung by to see if Clark could fix it. Of course, Clark was happy to help.

Now they stood behind the hardware store on a patch of tamped down snow. The dogs played nearby, their pink tongues lolling out of the sides of their mouths as Derek and Clark stood talking.

"While you're here—" Clark began, but before he could finish, he was distracted by a wet nose pressing into the palm of his hand.

He looked down, spotting a beautiful black and white husky looking up at him with her ice blue eyes.

"Oh, hey, Missy," Clark murmured affectionately, ruffling the dog's ears and giving her a scratch on the head.

Her full name was Mistletoe, but they called her Missy for short. He turned his attention back to Derek, who was shaking his head as he smiled down at the friendly canine.

"Anyway," Clark said with a chuckle. "While you're here, I got some of the supplies for the Hilton house. They're in the back storage room. Wanna see?"

"Absolutely," Derek agreed, walking forward to unhook the dogs from their leads. "After you."

He gestured for Clark to head in first, and the dogs yapped as they spun in circles around the men's heels, prompting both of them to laugh. It had been another slow day at the hardware store, so Clark had no problem with the dogs coming in with them, since there wouldn't be anyone for them to bother.

Plus, everyone in town loved Derek's huskies. Even the town grump, Rudolph Hutchins, was known to crack a smile when the silly dogs were around. He led Derek and the dogs around the side of the building, pulling open the door for them and allowing them to file in first before following after them.

The dogs burst inside, nipping at each other's heels as they played. Clark laughed and shook his head, watching Missy take off running around a corner as she chased after one of her brothers.

And then a high-pitched, startled sounding scream tore through the air.

Clark's eyebrows shot up as he and Derek shared a look before both men turned to sprint in the direction where the dogs had disappeared. They rounded the corner of the aisle at breakneck speed, and Clark came to a screeching halt as he took in the sight before him.

Sitting on the floor of the aisle was a woman he'd never seen before. Missy and Prancer, the dog that she'd been chasing, were jumping around the woman, licking at her face and hands while the woman held up two candles high in the air and tried to shield herself from the canine onslaught.

"Missy, Prancer. Heel," Derek commanded, and the dogs immediately came trotting over to him. They plopped down on their haunches, looking up at him with adoration.

The woman lowered her hands, face flushed, and her gaze locked onto Clark. She was so beautiful that Clark immediately felt his mouth go dry. She had chestnut brown hair that fell down around her shoulders and bangs that dusted across her forehead, accentuating her amber eyes. Those eyes narrowed at him, and she gritted her teeth, struggling to push herself up to standing with the candles she still held in each hand.

As he watched her, Clark was suddenly struck with the thought that he had seen her somewhere before. He knew that she didn't live in town—it wasn't that kind of familiarity. But he couldn't let go of it.

Just as he was about to ask where he knew her from, the woman opened her mouth to speak.

"Some of the candles on the shelf behind me fell and rolled down the aisle." She placed the two in her hands down and began to brush off the paw prints on her pants. "I stopped them from breaking when I fell, but I couldn't get them to stay put with the dogs jumping on me."

"I'll grab them," Clark said immediately, glad for the opportunity to be helpful.

The woman watched him as he walked down the aisle, his eyes scanning the floor for any sight of the candles. He barely registered Derek, who was still standing a short distance away in the aisle with the woman, gazing at her with narrowed eyes as if he too thought she looked familiar.

As soon as Clark reached the end of the aisle, he spotted the candles. Darting forward, he bent to grab all three of them where they were miraculously clustered together on the floor, halfway tucked under the shelves.

As he cradled the candles to his chest, he could hear his friend introducing himself to the woman.

"My name is Derek. I haven't seen you around Snowy Pine Ridge. Are you new here?"

Clark strode back toward where the two of them were standing. The dogs, well trained to respond to Derek's commands, were still sitting nearby.

"I'm Valerie," the woman said as Clark reached them and began setting the candles on the shelf where they belonged. "And I just arrived earlier today."

"Wait! That's why you look so familiar." Derek gaped suddenly. "You're Valerie Bernard."

The name caused a flash of recognition to shoot through Clark. Valerie Bernard, the romantic comedy superstar. Clark was the first to admit that the types of movies she usually starred in weren't his cup of tea. He'd always been more of an action or psychological thriller kind of guy. But he had seen plenty of trailers and ads with her face on it over the years that it had all been committed to memory without him ever realizing it.

Clark recalled one of those posters, where she had a brilliant smile plastered across her face, standing underneath a large clump of mistletoe while her handsome co-star smiled at her fondly in the distance. And as Clark glanced at the woman in front of him, he had to admit that even though she had been beautiful any time her face had come across his screen, she was even more alluring in person. Devastatingly so.

The woman, Valerie, was blinking slowly at Derek, color rising high in her already flushed cheeks. She shifted from foot to foot, looking almost uncomfortable.

"That's me," she answered, reaching up a hand to tuck a stray lock of shiny chestnut hair behind her ear. Clark couldn't help but notice that her hand was shaking, and he got the feeling that she didn't want to be talking about this particular topic.

"My wife, Lacy, is a huge fan. Maybe while you're here you could..."

Clark stepped forward, interrupting his friend mid-sentence as he extended his hand toward Valerie.

"My name is Clark Mitchell," he said, holding her amber gaze. "I'm the owner of the hardware store. Were you able to find everything you needed?"

A look of relief flashed across her face, proving to him that his suspicion was correct. He didn't know if she minded being recognized, couldn't imagine that she would at that level of stardom. But regardless, she definitely did not want to be talking about it in detail. Derek flashed him a curious glance, perplexed by the fact that his usually well-mannered friend had cut him off so abruptly. Clark could feel Derek's gaze on him, but he didn't turn his friend's way, opting instead to keep his gaze fixed solely on Valerie.

"I only came in for candles, actually." Valerie

pointed to the shelf behind her, where Clark's limited supply of them sat. "But none of these scents are what I'm looking for. Do you know of anywhere else in town that sells them?"

Clark knew of a few places, all of which had entire sections devoted to candles, room sprays, and all kinds of things that could help freshen up a space. But he found that he didn't want to name any of them. He couldn't put his finger on why, but Clark really wanted her as a customer. Or maybe he just wanted to see her again. Whatever the reason, he was as shocked as everyone else when he opened his mouth and said, "We can order some for you!"

Valerie's face lit up, an immediate reward for his words.

"Really?" she asked, her eyebrows disappearing as they raised higher into her bangs.

"Absolutely. We have a catalog up by the counter, I can point some out to you."

Clark pointed in the direction of the check-out counter, and deliberately did not glance at Derek. He could feel his friend staring at him in confusion as Clark and Valerie turned down the aisle and walked away from him. He heard Derek begin murmuring to the dogs that were still panting at his side, but as they got farther and farther away, Clark was unable to make out what he was saying.

When he made it to the counter, he walked behind it and then bent to retrieve one of his catalogs.

"What kind of scent do you want?" he asked, plopping it on the counter and beginning to thumb through the pages.

"Something sweet," Valerie sighed, as if the thought alone was enough to make her start to relax. "Everything you have on the shelf seems to be some kind of nature scent. Sandalwood, lemongrass, mahogany, that kind of stuff. Don't get me wrong, they smell great. But I'm looking for something that when it's lit it makes you think of your grandma's kitchen while she's baking your favorite dessert, you know?"

"So you want something cozy?" Clark asked, finally finding the first page that the candles were listed on.

"Exactly." She nodded excitedly.

He turned the catalog toward her, pointing toward the paper. "They start here and go on for a few pages. They have the name of the candle listed in bold and then the description of what scents are actually mixed together right underneath it."

Valerie murmured her appreciation as she began to look everything over, muttering things to herself like, "Ooh, blackberry cobbler," or "Apple streusel, yum," as she went. In the middle of it, she glanced up at him, her eyes bright.

"How long do they usually take to come in?" she asked.

"Usually, they take about two to three weeks, depending on the item and the warehouse," Clark answered. But when her face immediately began to fall, he quickly amended, "But I can do a rush order as soon as you let me know which ones you want. Typically, that means they'd be here in five to seven days."

"Oh, you can do that?" she asked, the grin returning to her lovely lips.

Clark nodded, a lie slipping off his tongue easily. "Sure can. I do it all the time."

"Okay, then." She turned her attention back to the catalog and began pointing at the ones she wanted.

She read off their names and he typed them into the computer at the desk, filling out the ordering form as he went along. Not once did he mention that ordering them in as an express shipment would cost him more than what was listed on the page. He didn't need to, not when he had already decided not to charge her for any of the shipping.

"And I think that about does it," Valerie said after naming the final candle in her order of nine. "It might be overkill. But I like having options."

"You don't have to explain yourself to me," he responded, giving her what he hoped was a soft smile.

"Well, then I'll just say thank you."

She grinned back at him, and it was a sight that sent his heart hammering so loudly that he thought for sure she'd be able to hear it as he pressed submit on the order.

"I'll let you know when they come in, but it should only be a few days. Where in town are you staying?"

"The Warm and Bright Hotel," she answered, and Clark nodded.

"I'll call there when they come in. I know Evelyn well. Actually, I know the entire staff pretty well. So they'll make sure you get the message."

He wanted to ask her a question, maybe even a hundred of them. Curiosity surrounding how a movie star found herself in Snowy Pine Ridge wanting to buy candles threatened to overwhelm him, but he diligently fought it off. Clark hadn't forgotten how nervous she had seemed when Derek had begun talking about Lacy being a fan. And he didn't want to be another name on what he could only assume was a long list of people who didn't respect her privacy. Because for the most part, when people found themselves in this town, it wasn't because they wanted to be noticed. It was because they wanted a retreat.

"That sounds lovely." She flashed him another award-winning smile before giving him a small wave as she turned toward the door. Right before she pushed it open, she threw a quick glance over her shoulder as she added, "Thanks again."

Clark nodded as she pushed open the large glass door. A blast of winter air swept into the building, making goose bumps erupt over his skin before it snapped closed. He stayed rooted to the spot, watching out the windows at the front of the shop as she wrapped her coat even more tightly around her and began walking down the street in the direction of the hotel she'd mentioned staying at.

A few, silent moments went by, filled only with the panting noises of content huskies. Clark barely even noticed that the huffing noises of their breaths grew louder as Derek approached, the dogs following after him loyally. He didn't look up as his friend came to stand beside him, still staring out the window long after Valerie had disappeared from view. Finally, Clark was interrupted from his vigil by the sound of Derek clearing his throat. He jerked slightly, turning to look at the other man.

"Well, that was something," Derek said, his dark brown eyes shining with excitement and barely concealed laughter.

"Isn't it, though?" Clark nodded. "A movie star in Snowy Pine Ridge."

"Oh, that wasn't what I was talking about." Derek smirked, walking up to the counter and leaning on it before raising his brow sardonically. "I'm talking about how you were almost tripping over your feet back there to get her what she wanted. 'I can rush order it for you, I do it all the time.'" His voice took on a different cadence as he mimicked Clark good-naturedly. "I've never seen you like that before."

"Like what?" Clark scoffed.

"Smitten."

Clark rolled his eyes. "Now you're just making stuff up."

"Sure, I am." That same, amused smile danced

along Derek's lips, and Clark just shook his head. When he didn't take the bait, Derek chuckled and then clapped his hands on the counter. "All right, then. I'm going to get going. Try not to swoon over our new resident movie star *too* hard throughout the night."

Clark didn't answer him, opting instead to just narrow his eyes at his friend while Derek and the dogs filed out of the building.

Once he was left alone, his mind couldn't help but wander to Valerie, and to Derek's observation of his reaction to her. Not that Clark would ever admit it, but he was quite smitten with the woman. Who wouldn't be? With a smile that shone so bright it lit up the entire room, he was sure he wouldn't be the only one stumbling over himself around her.

But the fact of the matter was, she was just visiting. People loved to come to Snowy Pine Ridge for short stints of time, but not a lot of them ended up staying. The town was what most would call "sleepy." Charming, yes, but the pace was slower than what some people craved, and that ended up chasing city folk away a lot of the time.

Besides, Valerie was a celebrity. Someone like her? She'd be there long enough to get her rest, to have some revelation about self-love and heal whatever it was that had brought her to town in the first place. Then she'd be gone, just like almost everyone else that rolled into town.

Because what could Snowy Pine Ridge ever offer to a woman like that?

CHAPTER FIVE

Shelley pulled open the door to Frosty's Shack, stepping into the familiar building and inhaling deeply when the scents of the delicious, greasy breakfast food floated up to greet her. She glanced toward the diner's counter, noting Louise standing behind it. Shelley gave the woman a friendly wave before walking toward her favorite booth in the far corner.

It was tucked in between two large windows, and had great views of Main Street, which ran through the center of town. It made it the perfect spot for her to sit and people watch while she waited for Rudolph to join her for breakfast so they could discuss some of the outstanding items regarding the children's showcase.

The moment Shelley sat down and made herself comfortable, Louise took out a notepad and began bustling her way toward the booth that Shelley now occupied.

"What'll you have today, love?" Louise asked, her friendly words at odds with her brusque tone.

The diner owner was frequently like that. She had a hard, gruff exterior, but once you got to know her, she was all warm and squishy on the inside. She might be hard as nails, but Louise cared about the people in Snowy Pine Ridge more than nearly anyone that Shelley had ever met.

"A coffee to start," Shelley said. "And then two orders of biscuits and gravy."

"Two?" Louise's eyebrows shot up in surprise.

"Rudolph is supposed to be meeting me here in a few minutes."

"That old grump?" the other woman asked, but there was no bite in her tone.

"One and the same," Shelley answered with a nod.

Louise just chuckled again, noting the order on the small pad she held aloft and then walking away to deliver it to the kitchen. She returned a moment later, pouring Shelley a mug of piping hot coffee before telling her the food would be out shortly and then hustling away to take care of another customer.

Shelley sighed as she wrapped her hands around the mug, letting the warmth rock through her as she lifted it off the table and to her nose, inhaling deeply. Coffee was her favorite thing about mornings, along with the feeling of peace that often crashed through her when she had a mug of it in her hands. It was something she planned to soak up as much as she could before Rudolph got there.

But apparently, the universe had other plans for Shelley, because a split second later, the door to Frosty's Shack was pulled open, allowing a frigid breeze to whip briefly through the restaurant before a frazzled looking Colette Hillis stepped through it.

Colette had an excited look on her face, her strawberry blonde hair glinting in the winter sun as she threw a wild glance around the restaurant. Eventually, her light brown eyes landed on Shelley, and Colette's lips tugged up to a wide, excited grin.

"Hi!" Shelley called out a greeting as Colette approached her booth. "What's going on?"

"You'll never believe what Derek and Lacy just told me," Colette murmured excitedly, stopping to stand by the booth Shelley occupied.

Colette was Derek's cousin and was also incredibly close with his wife, Lacy. She was a staple of the town and one of its sweetest residents, and she lived in town with her boyfriend, Zach McKnight. The pair had met when Zach had come to Snowy Pine Ridge a little over a year ago.

At the time, Colette had recently inherited the large house and connected property of the woman she had been a caretaker to for years. When Zach had showed up looking for a place to rent, someone had sent him in Colette's direction. Over the course of his stay, the two of them had ended up falling madly in love with one another, and he had made his "visit" permanent, even going as far as to open up an art gallery on Main Street. And just a few months ago, Colette had moved from the cottage house on the property that she had been living in for years, to the main house with Zach.

"What did they tell you?" Shelley prompted, looking eagerly at her friend.

"Valerie Bernard is in town!" Colette clapped her hands together and bounced on her feet, all but squealing in her excitement.

"Valerie Bernard the movie star?" Shelley asked, cocking her head in surprise.

Colette nodded her head eagerly, but somehow Shelley was still finding it a little hard to believe. It wasn't like the sleepy town had *never* had a celebrity come to visit before. But someone of Valerie Bernard's status? Someone that Shelley herself was such a fan of. And Colette too, if the fact that she was practically vibrating with excitement was any indicator.

"Derek said he ran into her at Mitchell's Hardware, of all places," Colette gushed. "Can you believe that?"

"I wonder what she's doing in town." Shelley tilted her head to the side in contemplation.

"Who cares what brought her?" Colette pressed her hands together beneath her chin. "She's *here!* In our little town! I think I'm going to go hang out at Sweet Thing Bakery today, just in case she stops by. I mean everyone needs coffee, right?"

She grinned at Shelley, who couldn't help but laugh at her friend's excitement.

"What's all this squealing about?" demanded a gruff voice from behind Colette.

Colette whirled around, and as she turned, it opened up Shelley's line of sight, allowing her to see the man who had just spoken. Rudolph Hutchins was standing a few feet away, eyeing the two women warily.

"Snowy Pine Ridge just got its very own movie star!" Colette announced, not noticing, or maybe not caring about, Rudolph's sour expression as he slid into the booth across from Shelley.

Just then, Louise approached the table, carrying a tray filled with two large plates of biscuits and gravy.

"Just on time, I see," the older woman mused as she approached, eyeing Rudolph, and then turning to Colette, who was still bouncing up and down on the balls of her feet. "Can I get anything for you? Although, it looks like you've already had plenty of coffee today."

"I haven't had any, actually," Colette quipped, blinking her large brown eyes at Louise as the diner owner adjusted the pencil that was stuck through her bun. "I'm just excited. Haven't you heard the news about who's staying in town?"

Louise shook her head, while Rudolph grumbled something along the lines of, "Gossips, all of you."

"You won't believe this, Louise. You really won't." Colette waved her hands in front of her face as she paused for dramatic effect. "None other than

Valerie Bernard is staying in town for a while. Derek saw her at the hardware store yesterday. Turns out, she's staying at the Warm and Bright Hotel."

"The romance movie lady?" Louise asked, and when Colette nodded, the two of them launched into an enthusiastic conversation filled with conspiracy theories on why Valerie was in town. The theories ranged from her possibly filming a movie close by, to deciding that she wanted to move away from the West Coast and settle down into a quiet life, and she wanted to check out Snowy Pine Ridge to see if it was just the place.

But Shelley wasn't fully paying attention to them. Instead, she watched Rudolph closely. When Colette had mentioned the actress's name, Shelley had just happened to glance at the older man across the table. So she hadn't missed the way his lips tightened at the movie star's name, or the way the light behind his eyes seemed to dim slightly.

She continued to watch him closely, wondering if he would let any other reaction slip, but he remained stone faced as he picked up a fork and began eating the food that Louise had brought out to him.

Maybe it was just my imagination, Shelley

thought as she continued to keep an eye on Rudolph, and he didn't show anything else but his usual, mild exasperation. She tore her gaze away from him, tucking what she may or may not have seen into the far recesses of her mind before glancing back at Colette and Louise.

The two women were still locked in conversation about the newest development in the town, and she had no doubt that by the end of the day every single one of the locals, and likely quite a few tourists, would be well aware of their newest, temporary resident.

Finally, the two women wrapped up their discussion of Valerie Bernard when Louise was called away to service another table.

"Well," Colette said as she turned her attention back to Shelley and Rudolph. "What do you think about it?"

"I think the girl likely wants to be left alone," Rudolph grumbled, not once looking up from his plate of food.

"Well, either way I'm gonna go down to Sweet Thing," Colette answered with a slight, affectionate roll of her eyes. "And you are all more than welcome to join me at any time today."

With that, Colette gave them a slight wave for a goodbye before turning and heading toward the exit. Shelley shook her head as she watched her friend leave, chuckling at the pep in Colette's step as she walked out the door and disappeared out into the blustery, winter day.

"So," Shelley said, turning back to Rudolph with a small smile. "What do you think..."

"Don't you go getting all excitable on me too," Rudolph grunted, cutting her sentence off. "I don't want to gush or talk about that girl. I want to talk about the kids' showcase, which was the whole point of us meeting."

Shelley paused for a minute, taking note of Rudolph's grumpiness. The man was usually less than pleasant, but it was typically in a quirky 'can't help but love him' kind of way. Now, however, he seemed genuinely on edge about something. Shelley thought about probing further, thought about asking him if everything was all right or if he needed to get something off his chest. But the moment the thought occurred to her, she immediately dismissed it. Rudolph wasn't someone that anyone in town would refer to as chatty. And Shelley didn't want to risk pushing him too far and having him leave breakfast before they got the chance to talk about everything they needed to.

"Okay." Shelley gave a quick, firm nod. "No discussion of Valerie Bernard."

Rudolph eyed her wearily, his dark brown eyes studying her as if looking for any indication that she was lying. When he eventually seemed satisfied that she wasn't going to talk to him about anything other than the showcase, he gave her a grunt of approval before launching into his plans for the rink during the showcase.

It was even more elaborate than the way he had explained it to her the other day after her ice-skating class. And she could tell that he'd spent quite a bit of time going over and over the logistics of the show to make sure that everything worked perfectly.

But Rudolph didn't speak about it all with the same gusto he had the other night. He was excited, sure. Especially for him. But there was something about the way that he spoke and the slope of his shoulders that told Shelley his mind wasn't entirely in the conversation.

Shelley filled Rudolph in on any updates to the choreography, and by the end of breakfast they had worked out a game plan for how to get everything set up and prepared for the big day. She lifted a bite of the biscuits and gravy to her lips, pleased with everything they'd accomplished in such a short discussion.

She opened her mouth to tell Rudolph, but she didn't get the chance. Because just as she was about to speak, he plucked the napkin he had draped across his lap up and tossed it on the table.

"Now that we're all done here, I'm going to head out. Thank you for breakfast," Rudolph said hastily, citing the fact that Shelley had told him the day prior that breakfast would be on her for all of his help with the upcoming performance.

Shelley barely had time to give him a quick 'no trouble at all' before he had turned and begun to stride toward the door. She watched after him, her mouth slightly agape as she tried to make sense of Rudolph's abrupt exit.

She glanced toward the counter where Louise usually posted herself, and sure enough, the no-nonsense woman was standing behind it, staring after Rudolph with an expression that mirrored Shelley's. As if sensing Shelley's gaze on her, Louise's eyes flicked over to her, and the diner owner raised her eyebrows and tilted her head in a silent question.

Shelley shrugged at her from a distance, although

she could tell Louise didn't believe that she didn't know why Rudolph had left in such a tizzy. But Louise would just have to accept it. Because while Shelley had a couple of guesses as to why the old curmudgeon had stormed out of the restaurant, she didn't want to go blabbing about it to anyone else. She knew that Rudolph wouldn't appreciate her talking to other people about him, and she would respect that.

But that didn't mean Shelley couldn't ponder about it herself. And as she sat at the booth, finishing her breakfast as the world around her went on with business as usual, she replayed the entire conversation with Rudolph over and over again in her head.

From the moment that Valerie Bernard's name was mentioned, there had been a marginal shift in the old man's behavior. And Shelley might not know exactly what it was, but she would venture to guess that there was more to the story when it came to Rudolph and with the A-list movie star that was staying in their tiny little town.

* * *

The winter sunlight streamed in through the pink, gossamer curtains that adorned the windows in Valerie's hotel room, pulling her out of her sleep. She blinked rapidly a few times, trying to pull her mind away from the dream she'd been having and plant it firmly in the present.

"What time is it?" she mumbled to herself, voice still thick and raspy with sleep as she rolled over in bed to glance at the small alarm clock on the bedside table.

Nearly noon. She wasn't surprised by that fact. Her sleep schedule had been decimated due to her many, frequent filming schedules. Whenever she was shooting for a movie, she always had to be up so early to start sitting for hair and makeup. And filming typically ran long into the night, leaving her often feeling completely and utterly exhausted.

So when she wasn't filming, she took full advantage of it. She'd often still stay up late, as she was accustomed to, and then sleep in as late as she'd like the next day. And the night before, Valerie had for sure stayed up late.

When she had gotten back to the Warm and Bright Hotel after her little adventure at the hardware store, she had been too excited to sleep. She knew that what would have helped her, even if just a little bit, would have been to have some candles to light. Valerie had even contemplated walking down to the front desk and asking if they had any that they wouldn't mind sparing.

But the last thing that Valerie wanted to do during her stay in Snowy Pine Ridge was draw attention to herself or to have others bend to her every whim just because they were fans of hers. She wanted normalcy, and normalcy she would have.

She swiped the back of her hands across her eyes, clearing the sleep from them before pushing herself into a sitting position in the direct center of the massive, four-poster bed. If Valerie had thought the room was lovely when she had first arrived the day before, then it was stunning now.

The way the sunlight streamed in through the window painted the entire room in various, wild hues of pink, gold, and red. She looked around the place smiling, thinking of how much she liked it there already, and she had barely had a chance to explore much of the town.

Her stomach gave a quick, loud grumble, announcing that it was more than a little ready for breakfast. A request which Valerie was all too happy to oblige. She pushed herself up out of the bed before tidying a few things up and then getting dressed for the remainder of her day.

She vaguely remembered seeing a cute little coffee shop and bakery the day before on her walk toward the hardware store. Her stomach gave another loud gurgle at the thought, announcing that it would be more than happy to settle for whatever Sweet Thing had to offer. The noise spurned Valerie on.

In no time at all, she was bundled up warmly in fleece lined leggings, her favorite crew neck sweatshirt, a camel-colored puffer jacket that dropped past her knees, and then a large fluffy, wool scarf. She pulled back the curtain of her bedroom window slightly, peering out of them at the snow-covered landscape beyond.

The good news was that there didn't appear to be any new snowfall. The footprints in the snow, as well as the snowman that she'd seen out front the day before all seemed to be completely intact, looking just as fresh as the moment they were made. But the bad news was that the air was still incredibly cold. Valerie could feel it seeping in slightly through the glass pane of her hotel room window. And she was glad that she had dressed in warm, cozy layers.

Not wanting to stall any longer, she walked out

of her room. The moment she stepped into the hallway of the hotel, she was met with noise floating up to her from the first floor. The closer she got, the more words she was able to make out, and she was surprised to find that it was all women's voices making all the ruckus.

Valerie crept down the staircase, taking them slowly so as to not disturb whatever was happening in the room beyond. When she reached the bottom, she peeked her head around the corner and her face instantly tugged up into a grin.

The tables that she'd seen yesterday that had been set out with coffee and treats had been stashed away, which wasn't surprising considering the late hour. But in their place now sat a round, fold out table. And at that table sat a group of women all around Evelyn's age, playing a rather loud game of poker.

Evelyn's chair was facing the entryway, and she must have caught some of Valerie's movements, because the woman's bright blue gaze flicked away from her cards and landed directly on Valerie. Her face brightened with a smile, and Evelyn gave her a small wave, which Valerie quickly returned.

Not wanting to interrupt the women's game any further, and also not wanting to draw any attention to herself, she hustled the rest of the way past the entryway and then out the front door of the hotel. The moment she stepped outside the cold air swirled around her, nipping eagerly at her nose, prompting Valerie to tug her coat a little more snuggly and readjust her scarf so it covered more of her face.

Once she was satisfied that she was protected from the chill, she set off on a brisk walk toward her destination. Despite the biting cold, something that she most definitely wasn't used to after living in California for so long, there were still plenty of people milling around the town. The town's residents were just as buttoned up as she was flitted from store to store, many of them weighed down with shopping bags. Had it been a little bit warmer, or if she'd been more accustomed to the chill like everyone else seemed to be, she would have stopped to admire some of the shops.

The town was truly idyllic, the kind of charming that would easily be featured in one of the holiday romances that was her favorite to film. The storefronts varied from beautiful, red brick with giant bay windows, to wood or stone that had been painted varying shades of pastels. Almost every single shop had a hand painted, completely customized sign that announced the business name, and she couldn't help but admire the extreme attention to detail, just as she had at the hotel.

But as it was, her cheeks were already becoming chapped, and so she didn't want to dawdle. Valerie was in awe of the people that she passed that all seemed to not mind the cold one bit, and she made a mental note to pick up a more heavy-duty moisturizer at some point. Because it appeared that the light stuff she used when out in sunny California wouldn't cut it in Snowy Pine Ridge.

She spotted the pink outside of Sweet Thing Bakery, the building that she had immediately taken notice of the day before on her way toward the hardware store. It was only about a half a block away, and as Valerie reached it and pulled open the door, she realized that she could even glimpse the hardware store from there.

Unbidden, an image of the man who owned it flashed into her mind. Clark, she thought his name was. Or something like that, a name with a rugged, small-town feel to it. She had liked the name, and liked *him*, if she was being entirely honest. He had been handsome in a way she hadn't expected to find in a sleepy little town like this. All dark curly hair and equally dark brown eyes. His beard had been close cropped, exactly how she preferred it, and a flutter erupted in her stomach at the memory.

"No," she whispered to herself as she stepped into the warmth of the bakery. The scent of apples, blueberries, and pastries all floated up to greet her. "Don't even think about the fact that he's handsome. You can't go down that path."

Valerie forced her mind away from Clark and all of his handsomeness as she unwrapped her scarf, finding it stifling now that she was in the warmer air of the bakery. She looked around, taking it all in and found herself smiling. Customers milled about at small, wrought iron tables, talking to one another eagerly. There was a beautiful glass counter and display case, filled to the brim with pastries that all looked and smelled mouthwateringly delicious. A chalkboard with gorgeous, scrawling script outlining the baked goods, as well as a variety of coffee and espresso baked drinks and their prices was affixed high on the wall behind the counter.

Just as Valerie stepped toward it, ready to feast her eyes on every single item before placing an order so big she could hardly carry it, a flurry of activity directly to her right caught her attention.

"Ohmygosh," someone uttered next to her, the

words coming out fast so that they all got jumbled together. "You're Valerie Bernard."

Valerie turned, spotting a pretty woman with strawberry blonde hair and big, light brown eyes that shone with excitement. She was bouncing on the balls of her feet, seemingly not able to contain herself before rushing forward to stand only about a foot away from Valerie.

"I'm Colette Hillis," the woman gushed, extending a hand for Valerie to shake, which she did gladly.

"Seems like I don't need to tell you who I am," Valerie joked.

"You really don't," Colette said with a grin. "I'm really glad you came in. I was hoping that you would, honestly."

Valerie blinked, her eyebrows lifting. "How did you know I was here?"

"Oh, my cousin Derek said he met you in the hardware store yesterday."

"The guy with the dogs?"

Colette nodded eagerly, her hair swishing back and forth as she did so. "Yup. That's the one. His wife, Lacy, and I are both big romance movie fans. So we knew exactly who you were the moment he mentioned your name."

"He did mention that his wife was a fan as well," Valerie mused, surprised that she wasn't feeling the slightest bit nervous.

"I guess you want to order, then?" Colette asked, pointing toward the counter and display cases.

"I do," she answered with a nod. Then, struck with an idea she grinned at Colette. "Would you mind going up with me and giving me some recommendations?"

"Yeah, absolutely," the other woman beamed.

Now that the initial meeting had occurred, some of the woman's vibrant enthusiasm seemed to have worn off a bit. And as they chatted while looking into the display case, it began to feel a little bit more like talking to a friend than someone who knew her from watching her movies on the big screen.

"The blueberry crumble muffins are really, really good," Colette said, pointing to one of the items on the first row. "And so is the apple streusel. If you're looking for something a little more savory, she has caramelized onion egg tarts."

"I'm sorry, what did you just say because that sounds heavenly?" Valerie asked, looking for the item that Colette had mentioned in the case.

The other woman pointed to it, laughing slightly. "It's right there."

They were interrupted by the saloon style doors behind the counter being pushed open, and someone bustling through them carrying a tray in each hand. The woman was tall, with blonde hair pulled back in a thick ponytail that cascaded down her back. She was wearing an apron that was dusted with flour and was humming slightly to herself before she noticed the two women standing at the counter.

She noticed Colette first, her lips tugging up into a friendly smile as she walked toward the display case to put the goods she was carrying into it.

"Hi, Colette, what can I..." Her words died out as her eyes flicked to Valerie before widening in recognition. "Oh!" The woman's voice was slightly too high as she continued speaking. "Hi there. I didn't notice you there."

"This is Sarah," Colette announced with a grin. "And, Sarah, you don't need to pretend. I've already told Valerie that I'm a fan, and that you are too. You can admit that you know who she is."

Sarah's round cheeks blushed slightly as she finished stowing away the pastries. "Well, I don't want her to feel like I'm ogling at her."

"Then don't ogle at her, silly." Colette chuckled.

Sarah closed the glass door on the case and then came to stand behind the register. Her smile held the same level of friendliness as she looked from Colette to Valerie and then back again.

"Well?" she prompted with a polite smile. "What can I get for you?"

"I think Colette has talked me into the apple streusel and the caramelized onion egg tart," Valerie answered. "And also, one of your iced vanilla lattes with oat milk, please."

"Iced?" Sarah's eyebrows shot up. "In this weather?"

Valerie shrugged. "What can I say? You can take the girl out of California, and however the rest of that saying goes."

Both women chuckled, and Valerie felt herself truly beginning to relax. She had been slightly nervous when she'd realized that not one, but both women knew exactly who she was and was intimately familiar with her work. Despite the initial enthusiasm on Colette's part, both women were talking to her and reacting to her as if she was any other person. And she found that she rather liked it.

So often in her line of work, she got branded as an 'other.' People saw her on a silver screen and assumed that they knew her, that they could say wild things to her in public or make assumptions about her because of a five second clip from an interview.

Social interactions could go awry relatively quickly. And Valerie didn't complain about it. It was something that she knew just kind of came with the job. But she couldn't help but find it nice when people treated her exactly like she was—a fellow human.

"Some of my favorites," Sarah said with a smile and a nod as she rang in Valerie's order.

Sarah announced the total, and Valerie eagerly handed over her credit card, leaving a big tip while she was at it. Colette placed her order for a pumpkin and peanut butter cupcake next, and then Sarah began putting the pastries on trays for the two women.

"Do you mind if I join you at your table?" Valerie asked Colette, suddenly not wanting to sit alone in the crowded bakery.

The other woman gave her a soft, welcoming smile as she nodded. "Of course." Colette turned to Sarah. "You can put those on one tray, so we don't dirty a dish. And come join us whenever you're done with the drink, if you don't have too much work to get done."

"I'm always down for a little gal time!" Sarah said with a grin that mirrored Colette's.

She turned her back on them, fiddling with the

espresso machine as Valerie followed after Colette toward the table she'd been sitting at earlier. As Valerie took off her coat and draped it over the back of one of the wrought iron chairs, she noticed the discarded wrapper of one cupcake and a half-finished cappuccino already at the table, along with a book resting beside them.

"How long have you been here?" she asked as she settled into her seat and plucked her pastries off of the tray.

"Since earlier this morning," Colette explained. "Sarah's one of my best friends, and I like to come here to read."

"It seems like a great place for it," Valerie answered honestly, and the other woman gave her an earnest nod.

"It is." She took a bite of her cupcake, taking a moment as she sighed with pleasure and chewed. Finally, when her bite had been fully swallowed and she washed it down with a sip from her mug of cappuccino before turning her focus back to Valerie. "Plus, my boyfriend is working on a big painting right now and has been at his studio almost all day. So I would have just been at home alone, and it didn't really sound all that great."

"Your partner is an artist?" Valerie asked as she bit into the caramelized onion tart.

Flavor exploded across her tongue and her eyebrows flicked up. Colette noticed the change in her expression and smiled.

"I told you it was good," she mused. "But yes. Zach owns his own gallery here in town."

"That's amazing," Valerie responded around a bite of tart. "I'll have to stop in and check it out."

Colette opened her mouth to speak but was interrupted by Sarah approaching. Her friend carried a large iced drink in one hand, and a mug of something steaming in the other. She set the iced latte down in front of Valerie before pulling out one of the empty chairs and plopping into it.

"So what are you lovely ladies chatting about?" Sarah asked as she took a long sip from her mug.

"Zach and his gallery," Colette answered proudly, but then Sarah made a face.

"Don't get me wrong," Sarah said, reaching over to pat Colette's hand affectionately. "I love Zach, but I thought we'd be talking about something a little more interesting. I mean, we have a *movie star* at the table."

She whispered the words 'movie star' like they

were naughty, and it prompted Valerie to throw her head back and laugh.

"All right," Valerie said once her chuckles had subsided. "What do you want to ask this movie star?"

Colette and Sarah's eyes both widened.

"You don't mind?" Colette asked, voice filled with awe.

Valerie shook her head. "Nope. I don't mind one bit."

The other two women shared a glance, identical grins pulling up the corners of their mouths before their attention snapped back to Valerie.

"What was it like working with Rory Strand?" Colette gushed.

"Were the tears in *Love You, Hate Me* actually real? Or did they use eye drops?" Sarah blurted.

Neither woman waited for her to answer before firing off question after question, and Valerie's eyes darted between each of them in turn.

"Is it true what they say about male movie stars having to do pull-ups before a shirtless scene to make their pecs look bigger?"

"What was your favorite movie to film?"

"No. Who was your favorite co-star to kiss?"

Valerie began laughing, holding her hands up in

the air, palms facing forward in a gesture of surrender.

"I can't keep up." She chuckled, shaking her head slightly. "One at a time."

Both Colette and Sarah's expressions turned sheepish before they started repeating their questions, one at a time this time, and they actually gave Valerie plenty of time to answer. And then, they asked many more questions as after that, everything from awards show gossip, her worst run in with the paparazzi, what it was like to do a *Vogue* photo shoot and interview.

They sat there talking for hours, and surprisingly Valerie didn't once feel the slightest bit tired or overwhelmed. The women, while interested in what she had to say, weren't treating her job like a superhuman feat like some did. They were excited about her answers, but it seemed like the kind of excitement to be learning something new. And the more Valerie talked to them, the more that she realized she liked them both quite a lot.

And they didn't just talk about her. She was able to pepper them with questions about the town and its residents. She learned that she absolutely had to try Frosty's Shack, and to also meet the owner, Louise. She had been told all about the dogsledding, and the town's giant Christmas tree. By the time they were wrapping up their conversation, with Sarah needing to leave to tend to a new rush of customers and Colette getting a call from Zach, Valerie had a long list of things for her to check out while she was in town.

The three women stood, clearing the table off and helping Sarah carry all of it back to the counter. Colette had insisted on walking back to the Warm and Bright Hotel with Valerie, telling her that it was on her way back home, and Valerie had to admit that she was grateful for the company.

While she waited for Colette to finish up her last goodbyes with Sarah, she took her phone out of her coat pocket. It had been in there the entire time she had been in the bakery, and she was only just now realizing that she had been so absorbed in her conversation with Sarah and Colette that she hadn't even thought to check it.

As she brought the screen of the phone to life, she only had one notification. A message from her agent, Florence Brennan. With a sinking feeling in her stomach, she unlocked the device and clicked into her messaging app and read what her agent had to say.

Hi, hun! Just checking in to make sure everything is going okay. When you left, you didn't say how long you were going to be gone. Do you know when you might be coming back? We miss you. Kisses! -F

"You all ready to go?" Colette's voice brought Valerie back to the present, forcing her to stop staring at her phone.

"Absolutely," she said, plastering a believable grin on her face as she locked her phone and tucked it into her pocket without answering Florence.

The two women fell into step beside one another, walking toward the hotel and with Colette pointing out many of the attractions she had told Valerie about while they sat in the bakery. Valerie nodded and made approving noises, trying as hard as she could to push all thoughts of the message out of her brain.

"Oh," Colette said as they approached the hotel. "I also forgot to tell you. I don't know how long you plan on staying, but two weeks before Christmas the whole town is putting on a Twelve Days of Christmas Festival. A lot of the businesses, bakeries, and whatnot are participating, plus there will be performances of different kinds. Carol singers, kids doing an ice-skating showcase, all that kind of stuff. You should go!"

Valerie considered this. Thanksgiving had just been last week, and they were in the final days of November. So the festival Colette was talking about was only a couple weeks away.

"If I'm still here, I'll come," she answered honestly, knowing that she wasn't in any position to give a full commitment, especially when she couldn't even tell her agent how long she would be away.

Colette didn't try to pressure her or inquire any further. She just told Valerie that it was fine before pulling her into a big goodbye hug in front of the hotel. Valerie relaxed in the other woman's arms, shocking herself as she did so. When had been the last time that someone who wasn't family or already a close friend had embraced her like this? With warmth and familiarity? It had been quite a while, that was for sure.

The two women said their goodbyes and then turned away from each other, with Valerie walking into the hotel and Colette sauntering off in the direction of her home. Valerie retired to her room for a bit, sitting in the large reading chair by the window and staring out at the snow-covered lawn below.

Valerie couldn't figure out why Florence's message had made her feel so crummy, but it had. From the moment that she read it, the small pit in her stomach had begun to grow.

She loved her life in California and loved her job. So why did the thought of going back make her feel ill? She took out her phone again and stared at the message Florence had sent her. And no matter how hard she tried, she could not come up with an answer to Florence's question. But even after only a day, she was starting to wonder if she might end up being in town longer than she originally expected.

CHAPTER SIX

"No, honey, a little to the right," Lacy called, staring up at Derek as he struggled to place the star on the very top of the tree that they were decorating.

Derek made the adjustment, looking down at his wife with a question in his eyes, seeking her approval.

Lacy grinned at him. "Perfect."

Her husband began climbing down the ladder he'd been using, careful to keep his balance as three of the huskies danced and howled around the tree. Piper, their nearly one-year-old daughter, sat on a blanket not far away, playing with a set of Christmas themed blocks and laughing joyfully at the yapping canines. Lacy's heart swelled with love as she looked between her daughter, her husband, and a few of their crazy pups, unable to believe that she had gotten so incredibly lucky.

When she had first come to Snowy Pine Ridge, Lacy had been more than a little apprehensive about everything the town had to offer. The only reason she even found herself there in the first place was because her grandfather, who she had never met, passed away and left her the house he had been living in.

She had heard terrible things about him from her mother, and Lacy's only intent had been to come and fix up the house so that she could sell it before going back to her life as a loan consultant in Saint Louis. But it seemed like the universe had other plans for her.

She'd found out the truth about her grandfather and her father, both two men who had been trying their best and who had worked tirelessly to help out anyone they could around town. Her grandfather, Nicholas, had even gotten the nickname St. Nick due to his overly generous nature. She still owned St. Nick's Place and had turned it into one of the premiere event spaces in Snowy Pine Ridge. And, in her grandfather's honor, she also still hosted the annual Christmas party for the town there every year.

Lacy watched as Derek finally plopped onto the floor from the ladder, turning to face Piper with a wild grin on his face. He rushed forward and pulled their daughter off the floor and into his arms. She squeezed him back with delight as he twirled her around, dancing and singing "The Christmas Song" at the top of his lungs.

The dogs, spurred on by Derek's over the top dance moves and Piper's excited squeals, began to howl along, joining in on the song. The noise was atrocious, and Lacy couldn't help but throw her head back and laugh. Derek's brown eyes landed on Lacy, lighting with mischief as he swept the arm that wasn't holding their daughter out toward her.

"My love?" he said, motioning for her to join them in their dance, which Lacy did eagerly.

When she was tucked into Derek's arms, Piper planted a big, messy kiss on Lacy's cheeks before returning to her babbling and squealing. And none of them stopped until Lacy's stomach ached from how much she had laughed.

"So did I tell you about the project I'm going to be working on?" Derek asked when they finally stopped dancing.

He walked over toward Piper's Pack 'n Play and set her inside it so that he and Lacy could begin preparing dinner. They often cooked together whenever they were both home, liking having a shared task that increased their time together. They moved the playpen and their daughter into the kitchen and got to work.

"No, you didn't," Lacy answered as she diced up an onion. "What are you working on?"

"Well, I'm sure by now you heard about the damage to the Hiltons' home?"

Lacy nodded, a pang of sympathy clanging through her chest.

"Matthew came to visit me and Clark the other day," Derek continued to explain. "And he's fixing up a house for them. He asked if we wouldn't mind helping out so the work can go a little faster. Clark is going to be donating quite a lot of the supplies, and labor as well. There are more of the guys from town helping out."

"That's amazing, honey," she said, leaning up on her tiptoes to press a sweet kiss on her husband's cheek as pride threatened to overwhelm her.

"I think so too." He gave a satisfied nod. "It'll be good to do something like that for someone else, you know?"

Once again, Lacy nodded, but she didn't take her eyes away from the vegetables she was chopping.

"Also, I forgot to mention—remember how I went to the hardware store yesterday?" Derek continued. "You'll never guess who I ran into while I was there."

"Barney the dinosaur?" Lacy asked, and her husband chuckled and shook his head.

"Even better." He paused for dramatic effect. "We ran into Valerie Bernard."

The knife in Lacy's hand stopped moving as her jaw dropped open in shock. Her gaze shot up to Derek, and she searched his face for any sign of a lie, but his brown eyes were open and earnest.

"Valerie Bernard, like... the actress?" she asked, still finding the information hard to believe.

Derek nodded. "One and the same. She was super nice too. And I guess Colette met her at Sweet Thing a little bit ago, and she had coffee and pastries with both her and Sarah. Said they talked for a long time. She texted me about it the moment she walked Valerie back to the Warm and Bright Hotel."

"What do you think she's in town for?"

Her husband shrugged. "Don't know. She didn't say while she was at the hardware store, and it doesn't seem like she said anything about it while she was with Colette and Sarah either. Colette invited her to the Twelve Days of Christmas Event, and I guess Valerie just said she'd go if she was still here. So who knows how long she's planning on staying."

"I hope she likes it here," Lacy mused before adding, "and I hope I get to meet her."

Derek chuckled. "Don't worry, I already told her you're a fan."

"I appreciate that." Lacy smiled up at her husband before the two of them fell into a companionable silence, working together seamlessly like they always did as they finished preparing their meal.

Soon, they were seated at the table with Piper between them in her highchair, everyone being fed their nightly meal. It was always quite the ordeal when Piper ate. Their daughter loved food. In fact, Lacy had yet to find any kind of food that the child didn't squeal with absolute glee over. Peas, carrots, mashed broccoli, even finely diced Brussels sprouts, Piper loved it all. And that night was no exception.

They spooned food into her mouth, the baby babbling happy with every single bite. When everyone was done, Derek stood up and kissed Lacy on the forehead.

"I'll do her bath and put her down to bed," he said. "I know you have some stuff you want to work on."

She nodded, smiling up at him fondly while he took their daughter out of her highchair and disappeared up the stairs to begin running her bath. She and Derek had cleaned most of the dishes as they cooked, so all that was left was the plates and silverware they had used to eat, and then to wipe off Piper's highchair, all of which Lacy was able to do quickly.

Satisfied with her nightly cleaning routine, Lacy shuffled through the house toward the downstairs home office. As she passed the staircase, she heard light splashing and giggles floating down to her from the bathroom, and she smiled. Lacy flicked on the light to the office, walking around the desk and seating herself before the computer. It took it a second to come to life, but when it did, she began pulling up her email and her calendar.

The night of the annual holiday party at St. Nick's Place was fast approaching, and while Lacy absolutely adored the party and this time of year in general, she now knew that she wanted to work hard and make it extra special this year. She did, after all, have a movie star to impress. And Lacy didn't have any time to waste.

* * *

Clark stood in the center of what he assumed was the living room of the foreclosed home, but without any furniture it was a little hard to tell. He turned around in a circle, taking it all in as Derek relayed to him what Matthew had planned not only for this room, but for all the others.

Clark nodded slowly, as his friend spoke, making a mental note of everything they would need to turn this vision into a reality.

"We're adding a bathroom onto the primary bedroom, that way Jeff and Margaret can have their own space. The kids can share the other bathroom on the second floor, allowing the first-floor bathroom to only really be for guest use," Derek continued to explain, pointing up to the ceiling.

Clark knew the primary bedroom sat right above where they stood, and he closed his eyes to envision exactly what it was Derek was describing to him. Slowly, the picture of what the house could be began to come alive in his mind's eye.

He could see it all, the way they would take a house that had looked more than a little forlorn and turn it into something beautiful, something the Hilton family would be able to grow and prosper in. Which would be a good thing for them, especially in the face of such adversity.

"I think it's really going to be something," Clark mused, opening his eyes and glancing back at his friend, who acknowledged his words with a swift nod.

Derek looked around them, noting the work that needed to be done before turning his attention back to Clark. "Want to start getting everything unloaded and in the house?"

Clark agreed, and the two men walked out the front door. In the driveway sat Derek's SUV, and right beside it was Clark's truck, the bed of which was loaded with supplies for the house, and all of it had been covered with a tarp to protect it from any snow that might have fallen while they were transporting or in the house. But thankfully, no new snow had fallen since the initial large storm, and everything had remained dry, albeit more than a little cold.

He reached forward, pulling the tarp off with a grand flourish revealing everything within. Gallons of spackle, sledgehammers, toolboxes, tins of nails, staple guns, wood for the new framing of the new entryways to each room, and more. it all had to go inside so the volunteers could begin work later that evening.

Derek let out a low, impressed whistle. "This is even more than what you showed me the other day."

"I found some more stuff I could spare in the back," Clark explained. "And I ordered some more. I'll be able to get the rest once I know for sure everything that we're doing and the dimensions."

They didn't say anything else as they reached forward and began hoisting supplies out of the back of the truck, loading up their arms with supplies until they couldn't hold anything else and then trudging through the snow toward the house.

"So that Valerie Bernard has Lacy in a tizzy," Derek said on their third trip out to the truck. He grunted with effort as he gave the large beam of wood he was lifting a tug, pulling it onto his shoulder so that it was steady enough for him to start making his way back toward the house.

"Is that so?" Clark mused, trying not to show how much just the woman's name made his heart beat a little faster. He kept his eyes focused on the two toolboxes he was pulling out from his truck bed, knowing that his friend would have no trouble noticing the way a blush crept into Clark's cheeks as he thought of the movie star.

"Yes," Derek continued, the two men falling into

step with one another on the way back into the house.

Sweat dotted along Clark's brow, the warmth of his skin caused by the effort of unloading the supplies directly at odds with the biting cold of the outside air. Clark was thankful when they stepped inside the house and set the wood down for a little bit of a reprieve. There was only one more load to go.

"I guess Colette and Sarah actually met her, had coffee with her and everything at Sweet Thing," Derek said as they made their way back to the truck. "Colette called Lacy immediately after. I guess they sat and talked for quite a while."

"I bet Colette was beside herself." Clark glanced over his shoulder as he pulled a container of nails and screws and a gallon of paint out of the truck bed. It wasn't hard for him to imagine how Colette had reacted. For as long as he had known her, Derek's cousin had been easily excitable. It was one of Clark's favorite things about her.

"Oh, she absolutely was. And Lacy can barely talk about anything else. She keeps saying she hopes she runs into her."

The conversation lulled as the two men set down the things they had been carrying in the living room of the house. Clark reached his arms over his head, stretching out his back as he turned his attention back to his friend.

"I'm not sure if I get the hype though," Derek said, clearly still talking about Valerie.

It took all the effort that Clark had not to allow the shock he felt at Derek's words to show on his face.

"Why is that?" he asked, and Derek shrugged one shoulder.

"Don't get me wrong, she's a beautiful woman," he answered. "But she didn't seem all that friendly when she was in the hardware store the other day."

"I didn't think she seemed so bad," Clark said, trying to keep his voice unassuming. But Derek's mouth ticked up in a knowing smile.

"Of course you didn't. You're so smitten with her."

Clark rolled his eyes. "Not this again."

Derek didn't answer immediately as his brown eyes moved from Clark's face to something behind him. Clark knew that he was standing in front of the living room window, but before he could turn or even ask Derek what he saw, his friend's smile widened even farther.

"Looks like you'll have an opportunity to show me just how not smitten you are."

Derek dipped his head, nodding behind Clark's shoulder, and Clark whirled to see what he was looking at. Trudging through the snow, her bangs slightly mussed by the wind and her cheeks pink from the cold, was Valerie.

"What is she..." Clark didn't finish his thought as he turned away from Derek, striding toward the front door.

He pulled it open just as Valerie stepped onto the front porch, and she stopped abruptly. Her eyes widened a bit in shock, like she hadn't been expecting someone to notice her arrival before she knocked. But the look only lasted for a split second before it melted away into a look of frustration.

"You aren't at your store," she stated forcefully, narrowing her eyes on him slightly. "It's closed."

"Yes," Clark answered with a hesitant nod of his head, not entirely sure why she was stating the obvious.

"The sign on the door said you would be open until seven in the evening. But it's only two!" she argued, her mittened hand flying around wildly as she spoke. Clark knew it wasn't the point, and Valerie would likely hate it if she could read his mind, but Clark had to admit that she was pretty cute when she was flustered. "How do you expect people to be able to buy things if you don't remain open when you are actually supposed to be open?"

Clark couldn't help it. He chuckled at her obstinance and shook his head slightly. "You're really not used to small towns, are you?"

"What does that have to do with anything?" Valerie asked, and he didn't know how it was possible, but her eyes narrowed on him even more.

"The store was slow, so I closed it." He shrugged one shoulder. "If anyone needs anything, they can call me. They know I'll run right back to the store so they can get whatever they need. It's kind of what we do around here."

"Well, how are people from out of town supposed to know how to reach you, hmm?" She took a step toward him, placing her hands on her hips. She looked so comical, her bangs sticking straight up as she glared daggers at him, that Clark had to bite his cheek to keep from laughing. "You live in a town known for tourism at Christmastime. How are people who aren't from here who need something supposed to find you?"

He gave Valerie a pointed, amused look. "You found me."

She blinked at him, seeming to realize that she had no argument for that, and had, in fact, just proved his point. A bit of the frustration fell from her face, the crinkles at the side of her glaring eyes easing a bit as her shoulders started to relax.

"I ran into Colette outside of the shop," she began to explain, her voice less accusing than a moment before. "She told me that you'd be here."

"And she would have done that for anyone else from out of town. All they'd have to do was ask," Clark answered with another small laugh that he immediately disguised as a cough as Valerie glared at him again. "I just finished unloading the truck. If you want, we can head back to the shop and you can get whatever you need."

Her expression softened even more, clearly caught off guard by his offer. "Really?"

"Really." He nodded in answer.

She seemed to contemplate this for a second, her honey-colored eyes flicking over his shoulder to the house behind him. Curiosity danced in the depths of that gaze, and only a second passed before she cocked her head in question.

"What are you doing here, anyway? It doesn't look like anyone has lived in this house for a bit. It looks empty through the window."

Clark glanced over his shoulder. He had half expected Derek to still be standing in the window, hands pressed to the glass and grinning as he watched Clark and Valerie interact. Clark could almost see his friend mouthing the words "smitten" at him and stopped himself from rolling his eyes at the image.

"It's a project me and a few of the other people that live here are working on," Clark explained. "Wanna see before we head out?"

Valerie's eyelids flickered, hesitation and curiosity seeming to war behind her honey-colored gaze. Curiosity, however, seemed to win out.

"Sure," she said after a brief pause, nodding her head toward the door behind him. "Lead the way."

Clark gave her an encouraging smile before turning and walking back into the house. He held the door open for Valerie to walk through it, noting the way that her expression continued to grow more and more confused as she stepped into the empty home.

"You know, you're still technically a stranger," she mused as she stood in the entryway, turning around and around to take in the derelict space. There were a few holes in the drywall, a bit of wiring hanging from the ceiling where a light fixture had been removed, and she paid particular attention to small droplets of red paint on the tile floor left over from the previous owner. "And there are plenty of horror movies that tell me going into this house with you is a very bad idea."

"Didn't anybody tell you?" Clark asked, cocking his head to the side and allowing his mouth to tug up into an uncharacteristically sly grin. "Not everything you see in movies is real."

She turned to shoot him an amused smile, which made Clark's heart rate pick up. But before he could say anything else, the sound of someone clearing their throat just a few feet away interrupted them.

Derek was standing in the doorway of the living room, eyes flicking between Clark and Valerie with an amused, knowing smile. Clark shot him a silent look, willing his friend to not say anything about the way that he was behaving. Clark wasn't what anyone would typically call a chatty person. He wasn't standoffish either, but he was careful with his words. But something about the woman before him made him feel like he could begin talking and never stop, if only just to keep her around longer.

"Valerie, you remember Derek," Clark said, pointing to his friend and hoping that by acknowledging his presence, it would stop Derek from embarrassing him.

Derek raised one hand in a small wave of greeting, which Valerie returned.

"I remember," she answered quickly. "The one with all the dogs, right?"

Derek nodded. "Sorry about them, by the way. You were gone before I could give you a real apology the other day."

Valerie waved a hand dismissively. "It's all right. They just scared me a bit. It's not like I expected a group of wolves to be running down the aisle of a hardware store."

Clark watched Derek as he spoke, remembering his friend's earlier words about how he'd found her a bit standoffish. Although he didn't know why, it suddenly felt very important to him that his friend change his original impression of her. So Clark waited, allowing the two of them to talk without interruption in the hopes that it would give Derek a little bit more time to form a solid impression, giving his friend the chance to warm up to her.

Derek laughed and shook his head. "Those crazy beasts wish they were wolves. But they are sled dogs."

"Oh!" Valerie's face lit with recognition. "You're Colette's cousin! The one she told me about who owns the dogsledding business."

"One and the same," Derek cooed, and Clark

didn't miss the slight swell of pride in his friend's expression.

"You'll be seeing me around, then. I want to try that out before I leave Snowy Pine Ridge."

"We'd be happy to have you," Derek answered, his eyes moving from Valerie over to Clark. His lips tugged up in another knowing smile as he said, "Speaking of leaving, I need to get home to the wife. So I'll head out. You two crazy kids take care now."

Derek said his goodbyes to each of them before walking toward the door, and Clark was thankful that Valerie's back was to him, and she didn't see when Derek winked at Clark before vanishing out the door.

"So what's the deal with this place?" she asked, drawing Clark's attention back to her.

She had her hands on her hips, looking around with open curiosity.

"We're renovating it," he explained, motioning for her to walk along with him as they ventured through a few of the rooms on the first floor. "There's a family in town whose house was damaged severely in the last winter storm. The snow caused the roof to cave in. And we're going to fix this place up for them, turn it into their dream house."

"And what are you getting out of it?" Valerie

asked quickly, and Clark stiffened, his steps faltering as he stopped to look at her.

They were standing in the middle of what was supposed to be the dining room, just off the kitchen. The narrowed, skeptical glint was back in her eyes, and he could see it in her face that Valerie truly thought that he was only doing this because it would benefit him.

"Because they're members of our town," he said, like it should be obvious. "Members of our community. We help our own around here."

The last bit of the hardness that had remained on Valerie's face since the moment she had walked up to the house fell, her lovely features relaxing into something a little softer.

"I can't believe that things like this are actually real," she said with a soft chuckle, shaking her head a little.

"Things like what?"

"Small-town charm, helping your neighbor, the golden rule, that kind of stuff. Stuff that I've only ever seen... well... in the movies." She huffed out a quick laugh.

"I guess some things in the movies are true," he said with a grin, and her answering smile felt like a reward.

"Am I going to get to see the rest of the place?" Valerie asked after a brief pause, arching her eyebrow at him.

Clark nodded, finding himself at a sudden loss for words as he turned and started showing her the rest of the rooms. In the kitchen, she walked over to the counter, running her fingers along the dusty surface while he talked about the butcher's block tops they were going to put on.

But even as he explained it, something in the back of his mind kept nagging him. Something about what Valerie had just said, about not seeing this level of kindness within her community before, and he couldn't quite let it go.

"What you said about this place," Clark began hesitantly. "Golden rule and whatnot. You aren't used to stuff like that?"

Valerie shook her head, not turning to look at him as she wiped the hand that was now coated in a thin layer of dust off on her pants. "I've only ever lived in California. My mom was a single mother, who had to work multiple jobs to make sure that I was provided for. And out there, in L.A., things have always been a little faster, a little more cutthroat." She paused and laughed again. "If anyone ever saw us struggling, they looked the other way."

"That's kind of sad," Clark blurted without thinking.

He immediately wished that he could take the words back, realizing that they were likely a massive overstep. He didn't know her, not really. Definitely not enough to comment on the sadness of her past. And as Valerie turned to face him, Clark braced himself for the onslaught that he was suddenly very certain was coming. But when her eyes met his, there was no awkwardness there, or frustration that he'd commented on something so deeply personal. Instead, there was just a quiet contemplation, like she had never really thought of it in that manner.

"It kind of is, isn't it?" Valerie answered, cocking her head to the side and giving him a grateful look before turning her back on him and striding down the hallway.

Clark followed after her, and when she stopped at the foot of the stairs he stopped as well. Valerie pointed up them, a silent question to which Clark just nodded in answer.

They began their ascent, neither one of them talking, and the only sound in the house were their hushed foot falls against the carpet. The silence wasn't an awkward one though, and that surprised

Clark. It wasn't often that people felt comfortable not filling the space with idle chitchat.

Once they were at the top of the stairs, he took her from room to room, watching the way her face lit up and changed when he told her what they were going to do with each, and by the end, Valerie was grinning from ear to ear.

"This is a really amazing thing that you all are doing for them," she said, her voice filled with awe as she looked back at Clark.

Pride swelled in his chest at her words, and he tried to stuff it down, but he couldn't quite get it to go away.

"They'd do the same for me," he answered, shrugging one shoulder like it wasn't that big of a deal. "If you want, we can get going and head to the hardware store now."

Valerie blushed, suddenly looking a bit embarrassed as she shifted from one foot to the other. Clark's brow furrowed as he watched her.

"What is it?" he asked.

"I'd almost forgotten why I'd come here," she admitted, glancing down at her feet. "But it seems ridiculous now."

"What does?" Clark asked, studying her features as she spoke. It was the first time he'd seen her nervous, and he found it endearing in a way that he hadn't expected.

Her blush deepened, and she didn't turn to look at him.

"Stain remover. I spilled something on the bedspread at the Warm and Bright and didn't want to bug the staff, so I figured I'd clean it myself. And everyone in town seems to use you as the general store. So it was the only place I could think to go. But after all this..." She raised her hands and indicated the house around them. "It seems a little silly to be worried about it in comparison."

"It isn't silly." He chuckled, shaking his head at her good-naturedly. "Stain remover is important. So we'll go get it taken care of."

Her eyes flicked up to meet his. "Thank you."

Her voice sounded so hesitant and so genuine that Clark felt his heart give a small tug, which he promptly ignored. The last thing he wanted to do was entertain it and give Derek more fuel for his teasing.

"No need. Now let's get going."

She smiled and followed after him as they made their way back through the house. When they stepped out onto the front porch, only Clark's truck was in the driveway. It wasn't a surprise. Derek had said that he'd be leaving. But it wasn't until the sight of the fresh tire tracks in the snow of the driveway that it really hit him that his friend had left him alone with Valerie Bernard. Clark was almost positive that if he got out his phone right that moment, there would be a slew of teasing, suggestive texts from his best friend.

"Need a ride?" he asked Valerie, pushing all thoughts of Derek and of what he may or may not have texted out of his mind. "You walked here, right?"

She smiled at him and gave a quick nod. "If you don't mind. I'm not that used to the cold yet."

Clark didn't comment on the fact that it would take longer than she was planning to stay to get used to this kind of cold, especially when she had grown up in California, as they made their way to the truck. He pulled open the passenger side door for her, giving her time to climb up into the seat and get settled before closing it gently.

And as he walked around the front of the truck, pulling open his own door and sliding into the seat, he tried as hard as he could not to think about just how much he enjoyed the sight of Valerie Bernard sitting on the bench seat to his right.

CHAPTER SEVEN

Shelley smiled to herself as she pulled her shoulder-length dark blonde hair back into a ponytail at the nape of her neck. She stood at the edge of the rink, looking out at some of the boxes and random items that she'd used to mark where the props for the showcase would be. One of her groups of older kids had a class that night, and they would be finalizing their own choreography and she wanted them to be able to see where the obstacles were going to be.

She turned and glanced at the clock on the wall and noted the time. Taking her phone out of her pocket, Shelley brought the screen to life, hit a few keys, and then brought the device to her ear. Rudolph answered on the third ring.

"Yeah?" the old man asked in lieu of a greeting.

"Hey, Rudolph," Shelley said. "Are you still all right to pick up the pizza?"

"On my way to Frosty's now. What do you want?"

"Three extra-large pepperonis, and then one Hawaiian for me and you to split."

There was a silence on the other end of the line, and it lasted just long enough that Shelley had begun to think that the call had been dropped. Just as she was about to ask if he was still there, Rudolph cleared his throat.

"Listen," the old man grunted, sounding uncharacteristically cautious as he spoke. "I don't think I'm going to stick around after I drop off the pizza. I think I'll just head home and leave you to lock everything up."

A small shock ran through Shelley at his words. She could have sworn that the old grump had begun to look forward to the classes that she taught. She most definitely had noticed him coming more to life each time he was around the kids, some of his general crabbiness falling away in the presence of the children.

She thought of that day at Frosty's, when the two of them had talked about the showcase and when Colette had announced that Valerie Bernard was staying in Snowy Pine Ridge. Rudolph had been off ever since then. He hadn't been particularly crabby or grouchy, quite the opposite, in fact. It was like the energy had just been zapped out of him ever since.

"Are you sure?" Shelley asked hesitantly. "I know the kids would love to have you."

"Thanks, Shelley. But I'm sure. I'll be there with the pizzas shortly."

Rudolph didn't wait for her to say goodbye as well before connecting, leaving Shelley standing there with the phone pressed to her ear and a perplexed look on her face. She had known that it was a low blow, bringing up the kids and trying to guilt him into sticking around. But she didn't like the idea of him moping about and spending a bunch of time at home by himself, which he seemed to have been doing a lot of lately.

The door to the rink was pulled open, allowing a quick whip of cold air to rush into the building and pulling Shelley out of her thoughts of Rudolph. Matthew smiled at her as he approached, and her heart beat a little faster at the sight of his blue eyes crinkling with joy. And behind him strode the lanky form of his ten-year-old son, Brandon.

"Hey, fellas." Shelley beamed, stepping into

Matthew's arms for a quick, comforting hug the moment he was close enough.

"Hey, Shelley," Brandon said, shooting her a grin as he trotted past her toward one of the booths so that he could sit and begin lacing up his skates.

Matthew chuckled as he watched his son, and it caused his chest to rumble against her cheek. She squeezed him a little more tightly, and Matthew must have sensed that she needed it, because he didn't let go of her. Instead, he planted a kiss to her forehead before craning back his neck so he could look down at her face.

"Everything all right, Shell?" he asked, brow furrowing with concern.

Shelley paused for a moment, wondering how to put into words exactly how her thoughts were spiraling.

"It's Rudolph," she began before slowly filling Matthew in on all of the details surrounding her concerns about the owner of the ice-skating rink.

She watched Matthew's face as she spoke, noticing all the minuscule reactions, and she could see the skepticism in his expression as she began to wrap up.

"You think I'm reading too much into it, don't you?" Shelley asked hesitantly.

"No." Matthew shook his head, his sandy brown hair glinting underneath the building's bright fluorescent lights. "I think there's every possibility something might be up. But there's also a possibility that there might not be. Rudolph is kind of just a strange guy. No one in town seems to know him very well, other than the fact that he doesn't get along with people."

Now it was Shelley's turn to shake her head. "He gets along fine with me and the kids." She wasn't sure why she suddenly felt protective of the old man, but she did. "You haven't seen him when he's with them. He loves being around the kids. I've even seen him cracking a smile or two."

Matthew shrugged. "Maybe he's just not feeling well?"

"Maybe," she conceded, finally taking a step back and out of her boyfriend's embrace. "But it feels like more than that."

"Please don't worry yourself sick about it, sweetheart," he said again, giving her a concerned look. "I'm sure he's just in a bad mood or something."

Shelley nodded slowly. She didn't agree with Matthew. She definitely didn't think it was just Rudolph being in a sour mood. She'd been around the older man enough ever since he'd agreed to let her start using the rink to host her classes that she could tell the difference. Besides maybe Louise, whom Rudolph seemed to tolerate the most, might now be one of the people in Snowy Pine Ridge who was closest to the old man. Or at least one of the people whom he seemed to begrudge the least. Except for the children, that was. And she knew that something about the situation just wasn't right.

Rudolph had been completely fine up until that day at Frosty's. But something that day had struck a nerve in the old man, and she had a sinking suspicion that it had something to do with Snowy Pine Ridge's new resident movie star.

Shelley let the topic drop as she and Matthew interlaced their fingers and walked over to where Brandon still sat. As they stood beside the bench, father and son chatting easily about everything he was excited to learn and practice that day, Shelley glanced toward the large glass entrance of the building.

Cars and SUVs were already pulling into the parking lot, and she knew that any second the kids would be in the rink, donning their skates and jittering with energy that demanded to be focused. She gave Matthew's hand a quick squeeze before walking over to the skate counter, taking down the few sizes she knew that they'd need and getting everything ready, placing them gently on the counter for the children to grab.

The kids trickled in, talking excitedly to each other as they rushed up to grab the skates and began getting ready for the class. And Shelley watched the door vigilantly, wondering when Rudolph was going to show up with the pizzas. She knew it was a long shot, but she'd like to get a good look at him while he was there, maybe even call a break in the skating so that she'd get the opportunity to talk to him. She didn't entirely know what was going on with him yet, but the one thing she did know for sure was that she was going to do everything she could to figure it out.

Valerie smoothed down her hair as she walked through the town toward the other bakery Evelyn had told her about called Baking Fiend. She had liked going to Sweet Thing, but it was a bit daunting when she thought about the fact that she already knew so many people there. So she'd opted to ask Evelyn for other recommendations instead, choosing to fly under the radar for a bit, just like she'd originally intended when coming to Snowy Pine Ridge.

A thin layer of fresh snow had fallen the night before, and it glistened brightly in the sun as Valerie walked, causing prisms of light to sparkle and shift. When she had first arrived in town, Valerie had found the town beautiful. But now that she had spent more time there, she was coming to realize that 'beautiful' didn't really cover it.

There was something deeper steeped into the town. It was in the way that people greeted each other when they walked past, in the way that the entire town seemed to hold its breath when it snowed, allowing itself to be cloaked in magic. It was how every business had jingle bells on the doorknob, meaning that at any given moment the entire place was filled with their tinkling. Valerie had never experienced anything like it before.

She caught sight of Baking Fiend, the periwinkle building had white shutters, and was wrapped in twinkling, pastel Christmas lights. People were spilling out of it, many of them holding to-go cups of coffee or bags filled with pastries.

As Valerie got closer, the smell of cinnamon, vanilla, and apples floated out the door, making her pause to sniff at the air. She was excited to try another new place in this town.

The person who had just exited the bakery stopped and held the door open for her as she passed, giving her a warm, friendly smile as they did so. For a moment, Valerie wondered if the reason they were being kind was because they recognized her. But there was such a sincerity lingering behind their smile, that she found it hard to believe. People being nice just for the sake of it was definitely something she was going to have to get used to.

She stepped through the threshold, the stranger letting go of the door and allowing it to shut softly behind her. Most of the tables were occupied, and the sound of people chatting eagerly amongst each other filled the air. It was cozy, with a Paris meets retro diner feel to it.

Spindly, black metal tables dotted the space and were surrounded by antique, wooden chairs. Pastel prints of the Eiffel Tower decorated the black and white polka dotted walls. It was about as different from Sweet Thing as it could be.

Valerie walked closer to the counter, her eyes roving over all of the offerings in the display case, when the sound of someone saying her name grabbed her attention.

"Valerie, hey!"

She whirled toward the voice, finding Sarah standing in front of her by the counter, clearly having just been in conversation with the woman behind it. The other woman, the one standing at the register wearing an apron coated in flour, had blonde hair that fell around her face in corkscrew curls. She had a round, kind face, and soft brown eyes that crinkled in the corners when she smiled.

"Hey, Sarah," Valerie greeted, surprised to find the owner of Sweet Thing Bakery in front of her. "How are you doing?"

"I'm doing really well." Sarah beamed. "I just came in to chat for a bit. Valerie, this is Mindy," she said, pointing to the curly haired woman behind the counter. "She's the owner of Baking Fiend, and a good friend of mine."

Valerie couldn't stop her eyebrows from shooting up in surprise, making the two women chuckle.

"A bit weird, isn't it?" Mindy chimed, and Valerie realized she quite liked the woman's quirky, unique vibe. "You think we'd be in competition with each other or something."

Mindy and Sarah shared a look before dissolving into laughter, and Valerie looked between the two of them in confusion.

"Why don't I get you something to drink and eat, and we can tell you all about it," Mindy said, still grinning as she looked at Valerie expectantly.

Valerie's eyes skimmed the display case and then the menu on the wall behind the counter. She quickly decided on the egg soufflé and bacon sandwich, and a blueberry crumble mini muffin, with a vanilla latte. Mindy rang her up, and then disappeared to get her order put together while Valerie ran her card.

"Mind if we join you for your breakfast?" Sarah asked, giving Valerie a tentative smile.

Valerie considered it for only a moment before nodding at the other woman. "Of course."

She and Sarah walked only a few feet, deciding to sit at one of the retro style black leather stools pulled up at the far end of the counter. From where she and Sarah perched, they had a clear line of sight to where Mindy worked on Valerie's drink.

"So," Valerie began, glancing between the two bakery owners. "You two aren't rivals or anything? I kind of figured you would be."

Sarah shook her head, pausing only for a moment as Mindy set a plate holding Valerie's sandwich and muffin in front of her before turning away to finish up her drink.

"We used to be," Sarah explained. "When Mindy first moved here, things were a bit tense."

"More than a bit," Mindy called out from behind the counter, shooting them a grin over her shoulder. "Sarah kept coming in here to scope me out."

"You came into Sweet Thing too, Little Miss!" Sarah teased good-naturedly. "She actually opened up around this time last year. And our heads got big. We challenged each other to a bake-off at the annual holiday party."

"You didn't!" Valerie let out a small gasp before taking a bite of her sandwich. It was delicious, with perfectly fluffy eggs, crispy bacon, and a jalapeño aioli sauce that brought the whole thing together.

"We sure did," Mindy chimed in, walking back over to the two women to hand Valerie her drink. "But of course, I messed up my eclairs, and had the teeniest, tiniest little breakdown. That's when Sarah saved the day."

Sarah rolled her eyes, but the smile never left her face. "I didn't save the day. I just said that maybe there shouldn't be a winner, and everyone could just enjoy all the other treats we made for them."

Mindy shook her head. "There was more to it than that. We got to talking that night and realized we had much more in common than we thought.

And that, instead of competing with each other, we could collaborate. We run complimentary sales, have a co-owned rewards program between both bakeries. It's been great, actually."

Sarah just shrugged, as if what Mindy had just outlined wasn't absolutely ludicrous and unheard of anywhere else in the continental U.S. Valerie looked between the two women, trying to find any hint between the two of them that they were lying, or that one of them secretly envied the other. But there was none to be found.

Any time one of the women looked at each other, there wasn't a hint of malice or jealousy to be found. Nothing but true affection shined on the faces of the business owners, and Valerie couldn't quite believe it.

"This place is like something out of a movie," she murmured in awe.

"You would know," Mindy joked, shooting Valerie a grin.

She had wondered briefly if the other woman had known who she was when she had walked in, but that comment definitely confirmed it. But even though Mindy had recognized her, she hadn't once treated her like it was anything special. In fact, the way that Mindy and Sarah were talking to her was as if she was already a part of their trio, as if the three of them had been friends for a while, and Valerie couldn't help but want to lean into it a bit.

There was a lull in customers as a few of the people at the tables filed out the front door and no new ones walked in, and Mindy used that time to take off her apron, walk around the counter, and have a seat on the stool on the other side of Valerie. The two women began peppering her with questions, asking how she was liking the town so far, and who all she had met.

Valerie gave them a run down, but the list was rather short. And when she got to the run-in with Clark and Derek at the hardware, their eyes lit up.

"Oh, Clark is lovely," Sarah gushed. "He's so helpful. Any time we need anything fixed, he's the first one we call."

"He sounds like he's more handyman than he is business owner," Valerie mused. "He showed me the house they're fixing up for that family."

Sarah and Mindy shared a pointed look before turning their attention back to Valerie.

"Did he, now?" Mindy asked, and Valerie could tell that the woman was trying to keep her tone light and inconspicuous. Not that she was succeeding. "And how did that come about?"

"You don't happen to have a boyfriend, do you?" Sarah blurted before Valerie had a chance to answer the other woman's question.

Valerie paused, taking the time to raise her latte to her lips and take a hearty sip, letting the liquid warm her from the inside out.

"Single as a pringle," she answered finally, and once again the other two women shared a pointed glance.

"Well," Sarah began, her words flying out of her mouth so quickly Valerie found it hard to keep up. "We have plenty of eligible bachelors here. You'd be surprised. We might be a small town, but since it's so close to great skiing and great hunting, and just outdoorsy stuff in general, men seem to flock to here. And a lot of them end up staying."

"Men like Clark, for instance," Mindy said, studying her fingernails as if she wasn't interested in the conversation, despite the conspiratorial smile that was tugging up the corners of her lips.

"Clark is *very* single," Sarah chimed in, waggling her eyebrows at Valerie, making her laugh despite the awkward topic.

"I'll keep that in mind," she answered around a bite of her sandwich. "But honestly, I don't know if I'm looking for that while I'm here."

"It might be fun though." Sarah shrugged one shoulder. "Getting dressed up, going on a date. Even if it doesn't amount to anything."

Valerie shook her head, but despite her protests, she couldn't entirely banish the idea from her mind. She felt the color rising in her cheeks as an image flashed in her mind, one of her and Clark seated across from each other at one of the bakeries, or maybe on a walk together through the town square.

She shook her head quickly, forcing the image to vanish as she turned her attention back to Mindy and Sarah.

"I'll keep that in mind," she said noncommittally, and the other two women gave her a soft, understanding smile.

Thankfully, they allowed the subject to drop, launching into a conversation surrounding the upcoming showcase instead. Valerie listened in while she finished eating, liking the way that the other two women didn't even have to try to make her feel included, it just seemed to come naturally.

They were planning their limited menu that they'd be offering during the festival, and they wanted each of their shops to tie in together, while still maintaining their own unique style. They asked

Valerie for feedback and ideas, bouncing things off of her as easily as they were with each other.

And Valerie tried her best to pay attention, she truly did. But every so often, when Mindy and Sarah were talking to each other and her thoughts had a spare second to wander, that same image of her and Clark would pop up in her mind.

Valerie had to admit that she found the man attractive, and also incredibly interesting. Even if she would only admit it to herself.

CHAPTER EIGHT

Mindy's phone buzzed in the pocket of her apron, jolting her attention to it as she ran the rag over the countertop to clear it from crumbs. Sarah and Valerie had left a couple hours earlier, and she'd been busy with back-to-back customers ever since. But now, as the afternoon was beginning to fade into evening and it was getting closer to closing time, things were starting to slow down.

She discarded the rag onto the countertop and pulled the phone out of her pocket. And the moment she swiped up on the screen and saw what the notification was, her heart gave a weary, saddened pang.

LANDON: *Hey, I know it's last minute, but I*

need to bail on tonight. I'm sorry and I'll make it up to you.

Mindy heaved a disappointed sigh before typing out a quick response, letting him know that it was okay, and they'd reschedule for another time. She had been seeing Landon Schaper for a few months now, but somehow things weren't picking up. They'd had plans to go on a date that evening, and just like the last two times they'd tried to meet up, it looked like this date was going to fall through.

Mindy supposed that he was nice enough, and when they actually got together, she had a good time, but she still couldn't help but feel like maybe something was lacking. She thought back to her conversation with Valerie and Sarah earlier that day, and how she and Sarah had attempted to play matchmaker for the movie star.

On the one hand, she really liked Valerie, and she liked Clark. And Mindy thought that the two of them would be lovely together. But on the other hand, she couldn't help but also want to save Valerie from feeling what it was like to be single in Snowy Pine Ridge.

Sure, the actress had no plans to stay in town for an extended period of time—not that Mindy knew of, anyway—but that didn't stop her from thinking about what it felt like to be here and be single. She and Sarah hadn't been lying. The town was absolutely full of eligible men. But so much of the town was coupled up, and they were all so madly in love that it almost hurt to see. Especially when you didn't have it for yourself.

And when she looked at her friends, at people like Colette and Sarah, at the easy way they loved their partners and the way they balanced each other out, she couldn't help but feel a pang of jealousy.

Mindy was getting to the point where she couldn't help but wonder if that was in the cards for her. She was trying her best to remain hopeful, and giving up on love wasn't something that she took lightly. But at the same time, she wasn't sure how much more blasé romantic encounters she could take.

"Get yourself together, Min," she said out loud, not realizing that there were still customers at two of the tables.

One of them shot her a worried glance, and Mindy realized how crazy she must have looked muttering to herself behind the counter. She gave them what she hoped was an encouraging smile and a small, apologetic wave before she turned her back on them and faced the oven.

Her phone was still in her hands, and she stared down at it as an idea began to dance in her mind. Not giving herself time to rethink it, she scrolled through her contacts until she came to Sarah's name, and then pressed call.

Holding the phone to her ear, Mindy walked toward her office in the back of the building, and Sarah answered the moment she walked through the office door.

"Hey, Min," Sarah said happily. "What's going on?"

"I was thinking of getting a start on decorating the bakery for the showcase," she blurted, looking around the office at the decorations she had already purchased and that were lying about still in their bags. "Are you free this evening after closing?"

"I sure am. I'll be over after I lock up at six."

"You're a lifesaver," Mindy gushed before the two women hung up.

She stood in her office for a moment, looking at the supplies that were scattered throughout the space and imagining what it was all going to look like. Valerie had helped them a ton earlier that day, throwing out ideas that both of them were excited to incorporate in their menu.

Mindy took a deep, steadying breath, banishing all thoughts of Landon and of her disappointment to the back of her mind before she strode back out of the office and toward the front of the bakery.

The final few customers had filtered out, and it was less than an hour until it was time to close, so Mindy decided to busy herself with cleaning up and beginning her closing routine. She sang to herself while she did so, singing Taylor Swift at the top of her lungs while she scrubbed down the oven and the counters and swept and mopped the floors.

By the time she was on her final step, boxing up the leftovers in the display case to sell at a bulk discount tomorrow morning, the door was pulled open, and Sarah strode in.

"Didn't you have plans with Landon tonight?" her friend asked in lieu of a greeting.

"Bailed," Mindy answered, allowing Sarah to lock the door to the bakery and flip her sign to 'CLOSED.'

"Again?" Sarah whirled to face her, exasperation written plainly on her face.

Mindy nodded. "Afraid so."

"Isn't that like the fourth time?" Sarah frowned,

coming over to help Mindy with the last of the boxing up.

"Third time," Mindy corrected.

"That's even worse."

They finished putting the leftover pastries into their respective boxes, storing them in the chiller for the night before Mindy nodded her head toward the back, indicating where the decorations were stored.

They made quick work of pulling the bags of decorations out of the office and bringing them to the front of the shop. Mindy pointed out a few of the things that she wanted to do, like placing the tree in the window and decorating it with the matching ornaments both she and Sarah had purchased the week before, and then the two women got to work.

They sang Christmas carols as they put together the tree, until Sarah's voice faded off.

"I want better for you than what's happening right now," she said, causing Mindy to stop what she was doing and glance at her friend in question. Sarah gave her a sympathetic smile before clarifying, "With Landon."

Mindy paused for a moment, giving herself a little bit of time to formulate a response. Finally, she blew out a hard breath.

"I know," she said, her voice low.

"I'm not saying Landon can't get there," the other woman amended. "Because Lord knows that I made a total fool out of myself in front of William when we first met. Not everyone can be perfect like Colette."

Mindy laughed, shaking her head as she thought of her friend. "Even Colette stumbled a bit with Zach in the beginning," she pointed out.

Sarah perked up at that. "Exactly. Not everyone gets it right at first. And maybe Landon just needs a push in the right direction. But you do deserve more than constant canceling and just feeling kind of okay about it."

Mindy nodded. "I know. It's just hard sometimes."

"Hard how?" Sarah scrunched up her face, clearly wondering what she meant by that, and Mindy blew out a breath before elaborating.

"Everyone I'm around, you included, is just so in love. I can't help but want a little bit of it for myself, even if it doesn't look exactly the same."

"It'll happen," Sarah insisted as she took a few steps forward and placed a reassuring hand on Mindy's forearm. "But you can't force it. Talk to Landon. If he's the right man, he'll rise to the occasion."

Mindy just nodded again, giving Sarah a

thankful smile before the two women turned back to their decorating. They changed the subject, moving away from Mindy's love life and instead talking about Valerie and how surprised they both were over just how *normal* the actress seemed. They chatted about Lacy and Derek, about how funny little Piper was, and about other friends of theirs in the town.

The longer Mindy spent with her friend, hanging up decorations and transforming the business that she loved so much into the Winter Wonderland of her dreams, the more her spirits began to lift. Mindy was beginning to see just how right Sarah was. She *did* deserve better than what was happening, and the right man would be more than happy to do what it took to make her feel special.

Now Mindy just needed to figure out if Landon was the right man, or not.

* * *

Clark stood, stretching his arms over his head and groaning at the ache in his lower back. A shipment had come in earlier that day, and he'd spent most of the morning bent over boxes and shelves as he unloaded everything.

"Last box," he grumbled to himself, taking out the box cutter and slicing it open.

As he moved the cardboard flaps aside, revealing its contents, a grin tugged up the corner of his lips. Valerie's candles were in.

He hadn't seen the movie star since the day that she'd come to the Hilton house, but that hadn't stopped him from hoping he'd run into her. Which, of course, he hadn't. So his next best hope had been to just wait until the candles came in, and now they had.

He picked up the box, a small grunt of effort leaving him as he walked it toward the front of the store and stowed it behind the counter, telling himself that he'd call the Warm and Bright in a bit to get the message to Valerie.

As he thought about her, and about seeing her again, he couldn't help but be curious. Of course, word had more than gotten around Snowy Pine Ridge that she was staying there, and people were abuzz with love for her movies. And while romance wasn't typically a genre that Clark was drawn to, he wondered if maybe he would enjoy it just because she was in it.

Without giving himself too much time to rethink it, Clark slipped his phone out of his pocket and pulled up the app for the web browser. The moment that it loaded, he typed in her name in the search bar and then let the internet do its thing.

As he expected, the very first result was her Wikipedia page, and when he scrolled down just a little, he found what he was looking for—her IMDB profile. Clark clicked on it, and when it came up, he scrolled through the carousel of all her best-known films.

He'd heard of more than he'd expected to, remembering their movie posters or the trailers that had aired when the movies were first released. He stopped on one that seemed promising, clicking on the icon, and pulling up a synopsis.

It was still, technically, a romantic movie. But it was shaped around the premise that she was a private investigator and fell in love with the man that she'd been hired to tail. The reviews called it a blend of *Rear Window* and *The Notebook*, and Clark was most definitely intrigued by it.

Just as he started to search the title, wondering if he'd be able to stream it anywhere, the door to the shop was pulled open. The bells on the handle chimed merrily, announcing the arrival of a customer just as surely as the blast of cold air that slipped through did.

Clark glanced up from his phone, and immediately his stomach bottomed out. Standing in the doorway, silhouetted by the sun, was Valerie.

"Hey," she said, immediately breaking into a smile when her honey-colored eyes landed on Clark and she walked toward the counter.

"Hi," he blurted, hurriedly clicking out of the browser on his phone so she wouldn't see that he'd searched her and stuffing it in his pocket. "Your candles came in."

Valerie's face lit up, and the sight of it made his stomach bottom out. He tried to play it cool as she reached the counter, leaning forward so that her elbows rested on it. But he was sure that if she paid close enough attention to him, she'd be able to hear his heart beating.

"Are they back there?" she asked, nodding her head to indicate behind the counter.

In answer, Clark turned his back to her and bent over to pick up the box. He hoisted it onto the counter in front of her, pulling open the cardboard flaps with a flourish.

"As promised," he said, and her grin widened in reward as her hand darted forward to grab the very first candle she saw.

Valerie took off the lid and inhaled deeply,

sighing as the scent washed over her. Clark could even smell it from where he stood, and he had to admit that it smelled pretty dang great. It reminded him of the blueberry cobbler that his nana used to make, and he suddenly understood completely what Valerie had said when she was reviewing the catalog. There really was something special about a candle that made you think of your grandma's baking.

"All right," Clark admitted, giving Valerie a crooked grin. "Maybe you're on to something."

He reached forward and pulled a candle out of the box, and she watched him with amusement as he sniffed it hesitantly. It was the apple streusel candle that she'd ordered, and it smelled like Sunday morning in the heart of fall at Sweet Thing Bakery.

"These candles really do smell great," he murmured, and was once again rewarded by Valerie beaming at him.

"I told you so."

Before he could say anything else, the door was pulled open again, grabbing both Clark and Valerie's attention. Both of them turned their attention to the newcomer, and the moment Clark saw who it was his face broke into a wide, happy smile.

Three children darted forward, one of them

skipping as they approached the counter a few feet ahead of their mother.

"Valerie," Clark said, turning his attention back to his companion. "This is Margaret Hilton, and these are her kids Stephanie, Jake, and Willow. The house you saw the other day? They're who we're fixing it up for."

Valerie turned to face them, her thousand-watt smile beaming in full force. Margaret, a matronly woman with a round, kind face, looked a bit caught off guard to be standing in front of a well-known actress.

"Valerie Bernard?" Margaret stammered, her apple cheeks reddening as she extended a hand to the woman in front of her.

Valerie nodded, taking the other woman's proffered hand and shaking it warmly. "I sure am. It's a pleasure to meet you."

"You were in *Yours Ever After!*" Stephanie exclaimed, jumping up and down on the balls of her feet excitedly.

The girl was only seven, and even though she was the oldest Hilton child, Clark was still surprised that she knew one of Valerie's movies.

"It's mine and Momma's favorite," the little girl gushed, turning her attention from Valerie to Clark, she began to explain. "In the movie, she plays a princess just like Cinderella. And she falls in love with a prince at a ball. There isn't a pumpkin carriage, though. It would have been cooler if there was."

Valerie threw her head back and laughed, and it was the first time that Clark had heard it. His heart started to hammer even harder, although he wasn't entirely sure how. It had already been going fast enough that he was certain he would land himself in the hospital.

"I agree," Valerie said to Stephanie, still chuckling over what the little girl had said. "A pumpkin carriage would have been much cooler. But I *did* get to ride on a pink horse."

"Was it really pink?" the girl asked, her bouncing becoming even more exuberant. "Momma said it was just special effects."

"Nope." Valerie shook her head. "It was pink. Through and through."

"That's so cool." Stephanie nodded in approval as Valerie grinned at her.

The woman turned her attention to the other two kids, giving them a wide and open smile. Jake was five and Willow was three, and both of them were much shier than their older sister. They stood on either side of their mother, holding her hands and looking up at Valerie with wide eyes.

"Hello to you two," she said, giving them a wink that made Willow giggle.

Clark's heart warmed. He recalled what Valerie had said about having to get used to a small town, how she found it hard to believe that people were truly as nice as they seemed in a place like this. But watching her interact with the Hiltons, he couldn't help but think that maybe Snowy Pine Ridge was already rubbing off on her.

Margaret turned her attention back to Clark, giving him a broad smile. He launched into an explanation of everything they had done over the course of the last week. So far, they were able to get two of the walls downstairs completely demolished, as well as the drywall taken down in quite a bit of the upstairs.

Margaret's face lit up at the news. Clark tried his hardest not to look toward Valerie as he spoke, but there were a few times where he just couldn't help it. She seemed to be listening intently, turning her head this way and that, and he wondered if she was trying to envision the updates that he outlined for the family.

There was a slew of thank yous, and when Margaret tried to pay for the items she'd come in for, Clark had waved her off. The family said goodbye to both Valerie and Clark before disappearing out the front door. And once the Hilton family had disappeared entirely from view, Clark turned his attention back to Valerie.

"I still can't get over what a nice thing you all are doing for them," she muttered, shaking her head in disbelief.

"Well, believe it," Clark answered with a grin. "Did you do anything like it in California?"

Valerie answered with a shake of her head. "I volunteered from time to time, and I donated to charities. But nothing like this."

An idea popped into Clark's head, and he didn't give himself time to second-guess it before he began speaking.

"Do you want to?"

Valerie cocked her head to the side. "Do I want to what?"

"Do something like rebuild the house? Something exactly like it, actually. We could use the extra hands."

Clark tried not to let his hopefulness over her answer show on his face as he watched her. She was clearly thinking about it, but for a moment she seemed like she was going to turn it down.

"I wouldn't be very good at it," she said, seeming hesitant. "I don't know how to do any kind of work like that."

"Doesn't mean you can't learn." He offered her what he hoped was an encouraging smile.

She paused again, shifting nervously from foot to foot before finally giving him a quick, questioning nod. "All right."

"All right? Does that mean you're in?"

"I'm in." She beamed at him, and Clark had to fight the urge to not sigh with relief.

"I'll see you Saturday morning then. Bright and early."

She didn't lose her smile as she paid for her candles. He offered to have them delivered to the Warm and Bright Hotel for her, but she waved him off.

"I had a personal trainer in L.A.," she explained with a light chuckle. "I am more than prepared to carry a box of candles."

"If you say so," he murmured, seeming slightly reluctant to let her go. "But if you end up needing help, just call the shop and I'll come out. The number is on the website."

She nodded, giving him a small wave before picking the box up off the counter and walking toward the door. Just like every time he'd been around Valerie, he stood stock still and watched her walk away, suddenly feeling incredibly hopeful for Saturday morning.

CHAPTER NINE

Valerie flipped another page in her book, her eyes skimming over the page in the thriller novel she had been losing herself in for the last few hours. After getting her candles from the hardware store earlier that day, she had gone back out to explore the town a bit more and stumbled into the book shop. Reading used to be something she loved to do, but when her career took off, she hadn't had much time to keep up with it.

She used to love reading romance novels, and that had been the first section she had started browsing, but none of the books that she had picked up caught her eye. Chalking it up to too many years spent acting in romance movies, she had begun browsing other sections, until finally, she stumbled into thrillers.

In her younger years, Valerie had never been one for action and adventure, aside from the one movie that she did that was an action-packed romance. But one of the psychological thrillers had caught her eye, and she'd been unable to resist the urge to buy it.

The first thing Valerie had done when she had gotten back to her hotel room was light one of the candles she had picked up earlier that evening and curled up in the oversized reading chair in the corner. It was now hours later, and she was about halfway through the book, finding herself enthralled with the twists and turns that the book was taking.

"If I'm not careful," she said to herself, "I'll end up staying up all night to finish the thing."

She pushed herself out of the chair, raising her arms above her head to stretch out her back, which had grown a bit stiff from the hours of sitting in one spot. She groaned at the relief it brought to her lengthening muscles, walking a few steps to stretch out her aching legs.

Just as she was about to curl back up in the reading chair, her phone began to vibrate. She whirled around, turning to look at the device, which was sitting face up in the chair that she had just vacated. The name Florence Brennan was bouncing along the top of it.

For a moment, Valerie just stared at her phone, debating on if she even wanted to answer it or not. But after a split second, her curiosity over what her agent was calling her for won out, and she darted forward and grabbed it, bringing the phone to her ear the moment she pressed *accept*.

"Hello?"

"Valerie, my dear," Florence began, not giving her a formal greeting, as per usual. "I would ask how you are, but the truth is I'm too excited. I have great news for you. Are you sitting down?"

"You want me to sit down for good news?" Valerie couldn't hide the hint of sarcasm in her tone.

"You're right, maybe standing up is best. Then you'll be able to jump up and down with joy."

"Florence." Valerie sighed. "Since when do I jump up and down? And what is this news that you have to tell me?"

"So I found a part that I want you to audition for," her agent began, sounding more excited than Valerie had heard from her in quite some time. "It's a bit more high stakes than the ones that you're used to. But it's a lead role in what is supposed to be a

Blockbuster hit. And the producers asked for you, directly."

"What's the catch?" she asked hesitantly.

"No catch. None at all. And at this point, the audition seems like it might be only a formality. You'd be starring beside Jamie Jameson, so you know it will sell tickets. And it's just the kind of thing that you need to show that nobody should be counting you out just yet."

Valerie began pacing the length of her hotel room, remaining quiet as she began turning over everything that Florence had said to her. If what her agent was saying was true, then she really did need this role. It sounded kind of perfect, especially with someone that she liked and respected as much as Jamie. They'd starred beside each other multiple times, and fans always went ravenous over their on-screen chemistry.

But there was something in the back of her mind, something that was keeping her from answering Florence right away. And that something was Snowy Pine Ridge. She was just beginning to get used to the place, feeling like she was only beginning to scratch the surface of all the things that she had to learn here. She didn't think that she was ready to leave just yet.

"When is the audition?" she asked, terrified that Florence would tell her it was in just a few days.

"December twenty-eighth," Florence said. "They're not making any moves until after Christmas, since half of their staff is scattered all over the country spending time with their families between Thanksgiving and Christmas. And look, Val, I know you're on this journey of self-discovery, blah blah blah, but at least promise me you'll think about it."

Valerie's heart lifted slightly. If the audition wasn't until after Christmas, that meant she had plenty of time to make a decision, to find herself here within the snowcapped mountains and find out what it was she truly wanted.

"All right," Valerie answered finally. "I'll think about it."

She and Florence made idle chitchat for a few more minutes before the two of them said their goodbyes, and when Valerie finally disconnected the call, she heaved a sigh of relief. She was glad that she didn't need to make any type of decision tonight.

It was weird for her to think that this news was causing such turmoil within her. Two weeks ago, she would have immediately jumped at an opportunity like this. But now? After talking to Evelyn, after meeting the people here in Snowy Pine Ridge, she was beginning to see that maybe there was more that she had to offer than just acting. Maybe there were things that she would find even more fulfilling than being on the silver screen.

Valerie wasn't sure what she wanted to do about the audition just yet. But the one thing she did know for sure, was that no matter what her decision ended up being, she still had quite a lot of life to live. And she intended to live it to the fullest.

* * *

Shelley pulled the soft, fuzzy blanket tighter around her, snuggling even further into her couch as she swiped once again on her iPad. Earlier that day she and Rudolph had set down and sketched out a few of the things for the showcase, using pictures of the actual rink to make marks and insert pictures of their ideas. And now Shelley was working on fine tuning it all.

The sound of Matthew and Brandon chatting excitedly in the kitchen floated out to her, warming her heart. Her two fellas had disappeared into the kitchen a few hours ago with promises of Christmas cookies to follow, and she could scent them in the air.

"For you, my dear." Matthew's voice came from behind her, and Shelley turned to face him.

He was smiling at her, his bright blue eyes sparkling as he held out a full glass of mulled wine out to her with a flourish.

"Thank you so much," she gushed, reaching forward to grab the stem of the wine glass.

She swirled the liquid around as she moved herself, making room for Matthew to join her on the couch. They sat side by side, with him throwing his arm over the back of the couch, pulling her into his side.

Shelley nestled into her boyfriend, appreciating the solid feel of him as her mind was pulled in a thousand different directions. She brought the glass to her lips, allowing the deep, rich flavor to seep into her, warming her from the inside out.

"What are you working on?" Matthew asked, peering down at the screen that she held in her lap.

"Stuff for the showcase," Shelley answered before she began pointing to all of the mockups that she and Rudolph had worked on. When she had finished, Matthew's face was lit up with admiration.

"I knew you guys had big plans," he murmured, his tone filled with awe. "But this is really going to be something."

Shelley shrugged one shoulder. "Rudolph came up with a lot of it. He has an amazing mind for things like this. He was absolutely filled with ideas."

"Which I never would have expected from him."

She chuckled, shaking her head slightly. "Me either."

There was a brief pause where the two of them continued to sip their wine, listening to Brandon as he sang in the kitchen before Matthew began speaking again.

"Are you still worried about him?"

Shelley nodded. "He is withdrawing more and more every day. It's like some kind of switch has been flicked off inside of him. He had been doing so good with coming out of his shell, warming up to the kids and even to me. But now it's just the same old Rudolph. Except now he might be even crankier."

Matthew's eyebrows shot up. "I didn't even know that was possible."

"Neither did I."

"You know you didn't do anything wrong, don't you?"

She turned her chin, glancing at Matthew. Her heart swelled with love as she looked at him, taking in his handsome, chiseled face, sandy brown hair, and blue eyes that so frequently danced with mischief. Now, however, they were filled with concern as he studied her.

"I know," she answered honestly.

And Shelley did know that whatever was happening with Rudolph wasn't her fault. But that didn't mean that it didn't hurt her. She hated thinking of the man reverting back to his old ways, especially with the holidays right around the corner.

Ever since she and Rudolph began working on the children's ice-skating classes together, she had come to care for the grouchy old man. More often than not, she found his moods and gruffness funny and endearing.

Brandon walked into the living room humming a Christmas carol under his breath and holding a plate that was piled high with Christmas cookies. He set it on the coffee table before collapsing into the recliner beside the sofa that Matthew and Shelley were occupying.

The three of them slipped into their movie night routine, with Matthew pulling up the streaming service that held the Christmas movie they'd agreed on and Brandon reaching behind him to dim the lights. The opening scene for *Elf* began to play, and as the noise of the movie drifted through the room, Matthew leaned toward her.

"Thank you," he said in a tone low enough that only she could hear. "For loving everyone as much as you do. Me, Brandon, even Rudolph."

"You don't have to thank me for that," she told him honestly.

Matthew just smiled and said, "I know," before pressing a kiss to her temple and turning his attention back to the movie.

Shelley tried but she couldn't pull her thoughts away from Rudolph. Matthew was right, she did adore the old man. If she was being entirely honest with herself, she had come to think of Rudolph Hutchins a bit like family.

She glanced between Matthew and Brandon. She and Matthew weren't married. They weren't even engaged. It had been hard for him to date again after losing his wife, and taking that next step wasn't anything that Shelley would ever pressure him to do. Not until all three of them were ready.

But that didn't stop her from seeing them as her family. They weren't bonded by marriage or by blood. But they were her family, regardless. And as far as Shelley was concerned, they always would be.

And she couldn't help but think that maybe Rudolph could use a little bit of family too.

CHAPTER TEN

Clark's eyes fluttered open, suddenly feeling wide awake. His room was still mostly dark, with only a faint light coming in around the edges of his curtains. He rolled onto his side, glancing at the alarm clock on his bedside table.

Seven a.m. Still an hour before he needed to meet Valerie at the Hilton house. But at the thought of her his heart began to pick up its pace. He couldn't deny the fact that he was excited to see her, and with the excitement currently coursing through him, there would be no way that he would be able to go back to sleep.

He pushed himself out of bed and flicked on the light before striding to the bathroom. Clark made quick work of showering and getting ready for the day, continuously telling himself that he didn't need to put a ton of effort into his looks since he was just going to be getting dirty when they worked on the house. But that didn't stop him from pulling on a pair of his favorite jeans and a black, long-sleeved t-shirt that he always received compliments on when he wore it. He'd just make sure to be extra careful while they were working.

By the time he was done, it was just before seven thirty, and he was struck with an idea. He strode from his room, walking through the house and grabbing the keys to his truck along the way. He shrugged on his thick coat, slipped his feet into his work boots, and then stepped out into the cold, winter day.

The air was milder than it had been all week. Still not warm enough to begin melting the snow, but it wasn't cold enough to immediately begin nipping at his nose. Which meant it was bound to be a good day to get a lot of work done on the house for the Hiltons.

Clark fired up his truck before expertly navigating out of his driveway and making his way toward downtown Snowy Pine Ridge. The moment that Sweet Thing Bakery came into view, he grinned.

The small parking lot at the side of the shop had

been recently salted, and he pulled into one of the empty spots without any problems. The moment he pulled open the door to the bakery, the smell of freshly baked pastries and coffee wafted over him, making his mouth water.

It was still early on a Saturday morning, so the bakery was mostly deserted. In fact, there were only three people inside of it. All of whom flicked their eyes toward the door and noted Clark's arrival.

"Good morning!" William called out from behind the counter where he was putting pastries in the display case.

Sarah and Colette were sitting on the stools that were pressed against the bar at the far side of the bakery. When Clark had walked in, their heads had been bowed together as they chatted eagerly with one another, but they had broken apart when they heard him enter. Now the two women were grinning at him, giving him identical waves in welcome.

Clark approached the counter, already knowing what he wanted to order to surprise Valerie with. William met him at the register, giving him a grin.

"You're in here early," he said, tapping at the screen of the register to bring it to life.

"Working on the Hiltons' house today," Clark

answered. "Valerie is supposed to be meeting me there soon."

"Did you say Valerie?" Sarah's voice flitted over to him, high pitched with interest.

Clark nodded before rattling off his order to William. He paid, and then the other man turned and began packing everything up for him and readying his drinks. As Clark stood by the register, he was startled slightly when both Sarah and Colette slid up beside him, one on each side.

"So what do you and Valerie have planned for the day?" Colette asked, and he could tell that she was trying to keep her voice from sounding too interested in his answer.

"I told you, we're working on the Hilton house today."

The two women shared a pointed glance while Sarah just murmured, "Mm-hm." Suddenly it dawned on him why they were so interested to know what he had planned, and he had to stifle a groan.

"You two," he said immediately, pointing at Sarah and then Colette. "Don't go sticking your noses into this. She met Margaret and the kids at the hardware store the other day and wanted to help out. That's all."

Colette held her hands up in front of her as a display of innocence. "I didn't say a single thing."

"It's just worth noting," Sarah chimed in. "That both of you are lovely, attractive human beings. It would make sense that you would gravitate toward each other."

"No one is gravitating."

"That's not what Derek is saying." Colette gave Clark a pointed look, waggling her eyebrows at him.

"Derek is a busybody," he grumbled, turning his attention decidedly toward William, who was very deliberately ignoring everything that was happening at the counter.

"I, for one, don't think it's a bad thing that you two are getting to know each other a little more," Sarah added, still looking at Clark.

"Oohhh," Colette trilled, clapping her hands together excitedly. "Who do you think will end up luckier to have met the other? Clark or Valerie?"

Clark rolled his eyes, trying his best to tune the two women out but failing.

"I think Valerie," Sarah answered quickly. "Don't get me wrong, she's great. And she has the whole movie star thing going, but Clark is one of the best men around."

"I think Clark is the lucky one," Colette argued.

"He does a lot of great things for the community. But do you remember all of the stuff she did for hurricane relief? She ended up helping a community ravished by tragedy."

"Good point." Sarah nodded. "But what about everything that Clark has done for the Hiltons and covering a big portion of the supplies?"

"How do you deal with this?" Clark asked William as the other man turned around, grinning as he held out Clark's order to him.

"I deal with it by agreeing with them. I think you're both a catch."

William gave him a friendly wink, and Clark could no longer hold back his groan as he grabbed his things off the counter. The two women, excited to have William also joining in the conversation, began to chatter at each other even more excitedly.

Clark shook his head at them, muttering a goodbye before turning and walking toward the front door. None of the three people inside did more than just give him an errant wave.

He placed the pastry box on the front seat, tucking the two to-go coffees into the cupholder before firing up his truck. He sat there for a moment, letting it idle as he thought about Colette and Sarah.

Yes, they were meddling with what was

happening between him and Valerie. But even though he found it rather frustrating, he also found it more than a bit endearing that they cared about him enough to put that kind of energy into talking about his dating life.

"You aren't dating her," he said aloud, shaking himself internally as put his truck in reverse and backed out of his parking spot.

Clark tried as hard as he could as he drove toward the Hilton house not to think of Valerie, not to let the fact that other people were now lumping them together get to him. But the one thing that he couldn't shake, the one thought that had rooted itself into the back of his mind and was refusing to let go, was that while he may not know her very well now, every single part of him wanted to get to know her more. Because everything he had gotten to know about her so far, he had absolutely adored.

* * *

Valerie's boots crunched over the snow as she all but ran toward the Hilton house. She was still so unused to getting up early that it was hard for her to wake up, even with an alarm. Which was exactly why she had slept through not one, but two alarms that morning.

She was lucky that her subconscious had realized that she was getting a suspicious amount of sleep and shook her awake. Otherwise, there was a one hundred percent chance that Valerie would still be lost in the land of dreams.

She turned the corner of the road the house was on, pulling out her phone and checking the time. It was eight o'clock on the dot. Somehow, she actually wouldn't end up being late.

As she got closer, more and more of the house came into view. Clark's truck was in the driveway, and he was leaning against it, gloved hands tucked into the front pockets of his jeans. Valerie almost stopped short at the sight of him, the way the early morning light was hitting him and illuminating his features.

His full lips tugged up in a smile at the sight of her, and her heart began to pound.

"You made it!" he exclaimed, pushing himself off of the truck as she approached and opening the door to his truck. "I brought something for you."

She had just opened her mouth to tell him that it wasn't necessary and that he shouldn't have brought anything when she caught sight of what he was holding.

"Is that a box from Sweet Thing?" she asked, her mouth immediately watering at the thought.

"You've got muffins, croissants, and breakfast sandwiches to choose from," he answered, thrusting the box out to her before leaning into the truck once more. He drew back a moment later, holding two to-go mugs of coffee and extending one to her. "And this."

"You are a lifesaver, you know that?" She beamed at him.

With Valerie oversleeping by so much that morning, she hadn't had time to stop in the lobby for coffee or to grab anything for breakfast. And her stomach had already growled three separate times on her run from the Warm and Bright to where she was due to meet Clark.

"Well, let's be a double life saver and go inside where it's warm so you can eat."

He nodded his head toward the house, and Valerie followed after him as he led the way. She was a bit shocked that they were the only people there. When he had invited her the other day to work on the house, she had assumed that there would be other people there working on it with her. Not that it would have stopped her from saying yes. In fact, the idea of spending some alone time with Clark was enticing enough that it might have actually been even more incentive for her to say yes. But it still would have been nice for her to be able to prepare herself mentally for their time alone.

Maybe I would have accepted being late and actually fixed my hair, Valerie thought as she caught sight of her reflection in the glass on the front door.

She had been in such a rush when she had opened her eyes and realized what time it was, that she had barely even taken the time to throw her hair into a messy bun before tugging on leggings and a sweatshirt and running out the door. With horror, it dawned on her that she hadn't even remembered to brush her teeth.

Valerie was even more glad for the box of pastries in her hand, at least eating something would serve to disguise any morning breath that she might still have.

"What are we working on today?" she asked once Clark unlocked the door, pushing it open and holding it for her so that she could walk in.

"I figured I could get you sanding the wooden banister for the stairs," he answered, not turning to look at her as he led the way to the kitchen and set the food and coffee down on the new counter that had been installed. "And I need to do some work on the windowsills today."

"Will anyone else be joining us?" She wasn't entirely sure what answer she was hoping for, but that didn't stop her heart from soaring when Clark shook his head.

"Probably not. I mean, one or two people might pop in and out. But I don't expect them to stay long. The main group was planning on coming out here tomorrow morning to do some more work on the walls and drywall."

"Gotcha." Valerie nodded, glad for the stall in conversation as he opened up the box and then held it out to her.

She stepped forward, taking a peek inside. She wanted to eat everything that he'd bought. But controlling herself and her voracious appetite, she reached forward and plucked one of the breakfast sandwiches out of it. The moment she bit into it she groaned with pleasure.

"They're my favorite," Clark explained, choosing the other breakfast sandwich for himself as well. "The sausage they use is chorizo, and it's perfect."

"I think this might be the best breakfast

sandwich I've ever had," she complimented around a bite of food.

The two of them were silent for a moment as they ate, and Valerie was surprised to find that she didn't feel the slightest bit awkward. She got the sense that, while Clark was often talkative around her, that he was a man that appreciated quiet moments, just like she did.

When they were done eating, they closed up the box, Clark assuring her that any time she got hungry she could come in and eat whatever she wanted from it. He walked her through how to begin sanding the banister, then walked toward the windows at the foot of the stairs and began his portion of their job.

"Have you always lived in Snowy Pine Ridge?" Valerie asked, keeping her attention focused on the sanding while he began working on the trim of the window.

"I have," Clark answered. "My family has lived here for generations. My great-grandfather is who opened up the hardware store, but even before that we had a long line of laborers and handymen in our lineage."

Valerie paused for a moment, letting that information ruminate. She couldn't really imagine knowing that much about your family, or what that must feel like to know what so many people before you did. Her own mother had been estranged from her family when she'd moved to Los Angeles. So Valerie had never really gotten the big family thing, let alone being able to recite all of the people that came before her.

A question flew to her lips so fast, she didn't have time to stop it.

"Did you always want to take over the hardware store? Or was it just kind of what was expected from you?"

The moment she asked the question, she wished that she could take it back. It was intrusive and rude, and she didn't know him nearly well enough to ask about stuff that sensitive. But Clark, for what it was worth, didn't appear upset in the slightest. No, when she threw a glance over her shoulder, looking back toward where he stood at the windows.

He had stopped working, his hand still pressed against the trim of the window. But he had glanced sidelong at her as well, and his expression was unexpectedly pensive as he thought about what she had asked. Valerie didn't interrupt him as she waited for his answer, giving him all the time that he needed to sort through his thoughts.

Finally, he shrugged one shoulder and just said,

"A little bit of both, I guess. Did you always want to be an actress?"

She nodded, turning back to her sanding as Clark also turned back to his work. "I literally can't remember a time when I didn't want to be some kind of performer. Even when I was little, I was obsessed with the movies. And on the rare days when my mom would be able to take me, I would ask her to show up as early as possible, as soon as the movie that played before the one we were seeing ended. That way, I could use the space between the first row and the screen as a stage."

"You did not?" Clark asked, amusement lacing his tone.

"I totally did." She chuckled, remembering it all fondly. "I would stand down there in that space that seemed so massive, and I'd look up at all the empty seats, imagining them filled with people. I'd sing, dance, recite passages from books that I could remember and act them out, even reciting some Shakespeare as I got older."

"That might be the cutest story I've ever heard."

She glanced over her shoulder, finding Clark looking at her with dancing eyes. She stuck her tongue out at him before asking, "What would you have done if you ended up not taking over the store?"

"I genuinely have no idea," he answered honestly. "I don't think I would have left town. I love it here too much, and I have no desire to leave. Maybe I would have opened up a bar, or an outdoor touring company or something."

"Small-town boy, through and through, huh?"

"Seems like it."

"What was it like?" Valerie asked, her curiosity ramping up all over again. "Growing up in a place like this?"

Clark ramped into a long explanation of life in Snowy Pine Ridge, and she had to admit, it seemed more than ideal. To hear him tell it, growing up in this place made for pretty much the perfect childhood. There was community and support, and a roving cast of colorful characters that had been present for his entire life. It seemed quiet in a way that Valerie didn't entirely know how to process.

After she heard all about his life, he began peppering her with questions—what it was like growing up in L.A., what are the best and worst parts of being a star? That question, at least, was easy for her to answer.

"The best part is easily the fans. It is the most bizarre thing to have people recognize you and genuinely care about the fact that you exist," she said earnestly. "It's heartwarming and overwhelming in the best possible way. But the worst part, and this part can get really, really bad, is the constant critiquing. Because I live my life in the public eye, everyone suddenly thinks that means that every facet of who I am is up for discussion."

She paused, taking a moment to steel herself before continuing on.

"Who I date, what I wear, what my body looks like. And people can be vicious, sometimes. While the job is amazing, and it's given me more opportunities than I ever could have imagined, it also can be really hard at times."

"You know, this might make you think differently of me," Clark said, his voice sounding slightly embarrassed. "And I don't even know if I should be admitting this or not. But I've never seen one of your movies."

"Not a single one?" she asked, her eyebrows shooting up.

"Nope."

She turned around entirely, then, sitting on one of the top steps and looking down at him through the railings. He hadn't turned around to face her, though, and she watched him as he worked. Valerie couldn't help but notice the way the powerful muscles of his back moved underneath the confines of his shirt as he continued to work on the trim.

"Did you even know who I was when we first met?" she asked, unsure of which answer she was hoping for.

This wasn't an unheard-of thing. Not everyone was super into romance movies. But it was infrequent enough that it made her take notice when it did occur. With Clark, however, she was ranging wildly between wanting him to be impressed by her, and also flattered by the fact that he possibly didn't know who she was, and he still had extended his hand and been nice to her.

"I did," he answered hastily. "I'd seen movie posters and everything, and trailers for your movies. But I have never actually sat down and watched one. And for what it's worth, you're even prettier in person."

His arm stopped moving as the last word fell from his lips and he turned around to face her. The blush that rose high in his cheeks matched her own, and she gave him what she hoped was a sweet smile.

"Thank you," Valerie said, not wanting to embarrass him more by commenting on it any further.

Their conversation died out as the two of them

turned back toward their work, with Clark moving on to a different window and Valerie moving higher up on the stairs. Without thinking about it, she hummed softly to herself, the melody of a Christmas Carol that had been on in the hotel lobby that had been dancing in her mind all day.

She lost herself in her thoughts, thinking about everything that she'd learned that day about Clark and the town as a whole. And Valerie was so deep in her own mind that she was no longer paying attention to what she was doing. One moment, she was humming and thinking about the way Clark had looked so cute when he blushed and the next second pain had erupted from her hand.

A hiss flew from her lips, and she dropped the handheld sander she'd been using, letting it hit the stair with a clatter. Glancing down at her hand, she noticed that two of her fingers were raw, with one of them scuffed and bleeding. In not paying attention, the sander had gotten away from her and went over her fingers.

Alerted by her sounds of pain, Clark came sprinting over. He bounded up the stairs in a flash and knelt down by Valerie's side.

"What happened?" he asked, his voice laced with concern.

"The sander got my fingers," she explained, holding up her hand to show him the damage.

He grabbed ahold of her hand, turning it this way and that while Valerie tried really hard not to focus on how nice and warm his hand was.

"There's bandages in the kitchen," he said, his brow creased with concern. "Let's go get you cleaned up."

Valerie nodded, pushing herself up off the stair she sat on with her uninjured hand and followed after Clark. The moment they entered the kitchen, he turned on the faucet and began letting the water get warm.

"The soap is antibacterial. Go ahead and wash it while I get the rest of the stuff to fix it up," he instructed, pulling open one of the cabinets and beginning to rifle through it.

Valerie did as instructed, letting the warm water run over her aching fingers before pumping on a bit of soap and beginning to scrub. It burned, but it wasn't nearly as bad as the initial pain had been when the sander had first scraped her skin, so she gritted her teeth and bared it.

When she was satisfied that it was clean, she turned off the faucet and grabbed a clean paper towel from the roll on the counter to dry herself with.

Just as she was finishing, Clark appeared back at her side with two Band-Aids and an antibiotic ointment.

He made quick work of spreading the ointment across her skin and bandaging her fingers, having Valerie flex when he was done so he could make sure they were secure. Just as she was about to thank him, when her hand was still in his as he inspected his handiwork, he did something that had her mouth popping open in surprise.

Clark, seemingly satisfied with the way that the Band-Aids were holding up, dipped his head and kissed the back of her hand with a flourish.

Valerie couldn't help herself. Once the initial shock of what had just happened, she threw her head back and barked out a laugh.

"What was that for?" she asked through the bouts of laughter.

"I guess that's more appropriate for royalty than celebrities," Clark said, the apples of his cheeks flushed with embarrassment. "But oh well."

He shrugged one shoulder as if it was no big deal, nodding his head back toward the area they'd been working in.

"Are you all right to work some more? Or do you want to call it a day?"

"I'm good," Valerie answered quickly, suddenly

incredibly reluctant for her time with him to end. "I'll just be more careful."

Clark nodded, leading the way back to where they had been working. And as Valerie fired up the handheld sander once more, running the thing over the wood of the banister in slow, easy circles, she couldn't help but let her mind wander. She focused on her work more than she had before, because the last thing she needed was more injured extremities. But while she did that, she also thought about Clark.

The man was a conundrum. Shy at times, bold at others. He laughed easily and had a wicked sense of humor. Everything that she learned about him had her more and more interested. And she would have to be blind not to notice how attractive he was.

Valerie's head snapped up, her eyes darting away from the tool in her hands to Clark for just a split second before going back to her work, a sinking sensation hollowing out her stomach as realization washed over her. In her search to belong a little more in Snowy Pine Ridge, she had somehow found something else entirely different. And that something was a crush on Clark Mitchell.

CHAPTER ELEVEN

Shelley turned the key on the Zamboni, shutting the giant machine down, the absence of its loud hum making her ears ring for a second. She climbed down from the chair, hopping down onto the ground before walking forward and taking a look out at the rink. The ice was perfect and gleaming, just begging to be skated on. And as was occurring so often these days, Rudolph was nowhere to be found.

A bolt of concern flashed through her once again, so strong that Shelley had trouble stifling it down. She felt like the old man was growing more and more withdrawn by the day, and no matter what she did, she couldn't figure out the cause of it.

Shelley glanced at the far side of the rink, eyes landing immediately at the large digital clock. There was still thirty minutes until the class began, which meant Rudolph would usually be behind the counter with the skates, spraying them down with another layer of disinfectant and murmuring about germy children while he smiled to himself. But of course, the area was empty.

Wondering where he was, she walked around the ice rink, glancing everywhere she could think of for any sign of him. But there was none. When she had finally ran out of places to look, she realized that if he was there, there was only one place left, and that was in his office.

Shelley turned down the long hallway at the back of the building, the one with doors lining either side. She knew this area by heart, knowing which doors led to cleaning supplies, which led to the bathrooms, and which led to storage. But it was the door at the far end that she was looking for.

She didn't knock, knowing that if he was inside, the grumpy older man would more than likely not answer her regardless. So instead, she just grabbed the doorknob and gave it a twist. It turned easily, the door swinging open with a low creak as it let her in.

Her eyes scraped over the small, cramped space, immediately noticing that he wasn't there. Shelley let out a sigh of disappointment. She wasn't even sure what she had been going to say to Rudolph.

She knew that confronting him about how much he was regressing likely wasn't the best course of action, but she was tired of waiting for him to snap out of it. Shelley was just about to close the door and try to think of a plan to get Rudolph back out of his shell when something caught her eye.

There was a small, white piece of paper lying face down on the floor by his desk. But it looked like it had been swept off by an errant gust of wind, likely even when she had opened the door just moments before. Scrawling handwriting was on the paper, but from where she was standing, she couldn't make out what it said.

Shelley threw a glance over her shoulder, making sure that no one was around to see her as she darted forward. She didn't want Rudolph to come in and think that she had been snooping through his things, so she knew it was best if she put the paper back up on his desk.

But as she closed in on it and then bent down to pick it up, she realized that it wasn't paper at all. The feel of it was waxy, and the white of it was a bit discolored with age. And as the texture and the print on it began to register, she realized that what she was looking at was the back of a picture.

You can skate circles around any guy in town. I love you. —Paula.

That was what had been written on the back of it, and Shelley's brows knitted together in confusion as she read them. Curiosity flared within her, and even though she knew that Rudolph probably wouldn't like it, she flipped the picture over.

It was an old one, that much was for sure, with the colors muted and the edges crinkled from age. There was a young man and woman in the picture, with their arms slung around each other's shoulders as they grinned widely at the camera. The man was definitely a young Rudolph, but Shelley had no idea who the woman might be. There was no one in town named Paula, not that she was aware of. But still, there was something about the woman's dark hair and the shape of her face that looked vaguely familiar.

Had this picture been taken in Snowy Pine Ridge? Or somewhere else? She peered at the background, trying to get a clue as to the location, but it was too vague and out of focus to give her any real hints.

She wondered if perhaps this was from the old

man's hockey days, and she was about to go digging for more clues when the sound of a door slamming shut somewhere in the rink brought her to her senses. With a jolt, she set the picture down on Rudolph's desk and hurried out the door, shutting it gently behind her.

She wasn't sure if it was the man himself, or if it was one of the kids showing up early to their class. But the one thing that Shelley knew for sure was that she didn't want anyone to know that she had been thinking about snooping in Rudolph Hutchins' office.

Disappearing into the bathroom, she stopped at the sink and turned it on, washing her hands just for something to do. Shelley had been in Rudolph's office a thousand times before, and she had never seen that picture. Not once. So that meant it was a new addition to the desk.

Could it have something to do with Rudolph's sudden melancholy? Did it have something to do with the woman in it?

Shelley blew out a breath as she finished washing her hands and then ran them under the air dryer, no closer to an answer by the time she pushed the door open once more. She may have no idea what was going on with the old man. But she did know one thing—she was going to do whatever it took to find out.

*　*　*

Clark laughed, shaking his head at Valerie. It was Monday night, and this was their third day in a row working on the Hilton house. If he had thought that things had been easy with her when they'd first started working together on Saturday, then they were even more smooth sailing come Monday.

Yesterday there had been other people on site, so he hadn't gotten to talk to her as much as he'd liked. But that hadn't stopped him from stealing all the conversation that he could. Tonight, however, they had the place to themselves, and as much as he liked the other people that were helping out, he was glad that it was just the two of them.

"You can't be serious?" he asked, as Valerie continued to snort laugh. "You really fell off the stage?"

"I did. Headfirst, straight into the crowd." Valerie nodded, honey eyes dancing with humor.

He shook his head at her, easily imagining the tale that she was weaving. Clark could see it in his mind's eye, the vision of her at an awards show walking up the stairs, and just as her foot came down on the stage the heel snapped off, sending her tumbling over. He may not have kept up with much in pop culture, but even he was surprised that he hadn't heard of it, that was something that usually people would have loved to gossip about.

"Now you," she urged. "You tell me your most embarrassing moment."

Clark scrunched up his face, thinking for a moment before shrugging. "I don't think I have one. I don't get embarrassed easily."

Valerie rolled her eyes good-naturedly. "Oh, please," she scoffed. "Have you seen how easy you blush?"

As if on cue, Clark felt heat rise in his cheeks, and a satisfied smirk darted across Valerie's face. She raised her eyebrows at him, clearly thinking, *See? Told you so.*

He didn't answer her though, not when the reason why he blushed around her so easily was sitting on the tip of his tongue. He didn't get flustered around her because he was embarrassed. He got flustered around her because he found her so beautiful and charming that he couldn't think straight. But it wasn't like he could tell her that.

So instead, Clark just shrugged again, and opted for changing the subject.

"What did your family say about it?" he asked, referencing the story that she had just told.

Valerie grew quiet for a moment, long enough that he started to panic that he had misstepped. When she finally began speaking, her voice was pensive.

"It was actually right after my mom died," she said, her voice thick. "I think that was part of the reason it happened, actually. I hadn't had time to go out and buy the shoes my stylist had recommended, and so I grabbed an old pair that were similar from my closet. I was so tired that I was walking really hard on them, and I think that's why the heel broke."

Clark's heart gave a pang of sadness at her words. "I didn't know she was gone. I'm so sorry."

Valerie had talked about her mother with him before, but she had never told him that the woman had passed away. If he'd known, he never would have asked.

"It's all right," she answered softly. "I've dealt with it. I still miss her a lot. But that's life."

"And your dad?" he asked, worried that he was overstepping by asking, but Valerie just shrugged.

"We aren't close. He and my mom separated

when I was really, really young. I've seen him a few times here and there throughout my life. But not enough for him to be a fixture."

"He never reached out after you got famous?"

She shook her head. "I don't think he cared very much, if I'm being honest."

Clark couldn't help but hurt for the woman before him as she told him her story. He thought of his own family—his mother and father who, at that very moment, were likely having dinner just a few miles away. He had never known what it was like not to have family hovering over him, to not have the support that they provided, and it was something he didn't like to think about.

And yet, there Valerie was, sitting in front of him talking about being a type of alone that he couldn't even fathom, all like it was nothing.

"Did I tell you my agent called me about a new movie?" Valerie asked, clearly eager to change the subject.

Clark, more than happy to give her whatever she wanted in that moment, shook his head. "Nope. Tell me all about it."

And she did. The words began rolling off of her tongue quickly as she recited everything she knew about the role and the offer that came with it. At some point, Clark stopped working and walked over and sat beside her, both of them sitting shoulder to shoulder as she continued her story. And as Valerie opened up to him about how torn she was about it, how much it hurt her sometimes to think that she was "aging out" of Hollywood and leading lady roles and how this might be her last chance to prove to them that she wasn't done yet, his heart ached for her in an entirely new way.

"There's one part of me that wants to take it," Valerie said as she finished telling him all about the new role. "Just to prove to everyone that I have it in me. But there's another part of me that doesn't want to be in this world anymore. I'm learning so much here, and I think there might be more to my life than everything I've done so far."

Clark stared at her, his chest filling with awe. "I know I haven't known you very long," he began, his voice low and reverent. "But I can't imagine even half of the stuff that you've gone through. You might be one of the strongest people I've ever met."

Valerie's amber eyes glowed as they held each other's gazes. And, as if in slow motion, she began to bend toward him. Clark didn't give himself time to second-guess what was happening as he dipped his head, meeting her in the middle. Warmth flowed through him the moment that their lips touched, and he realized that although he might have had plenty of kisses in his lifetime, there had never been a single one quite like this.

The kiss lasted for a long moment, and by the time they pulled away, his heart was racing. Clark reached up a shaking hand, brushing a bit of hair back behind Valerie's ear, and her eyes fluttered closed as she leaned into his touch.

She nuzzled against his palm for a few heartbeats before her eyes opened once more. But where there had been warmth in her luminous irises just a short time before, there was now uncertainty lingering in her gaze, and Clark's brows dipped together in concern.

"What's wrong?" he asked.

"Nothing, it's just..." Valerie paused, biting her bottom lip. He could tell that she was considering her words carefully, and he didn't want to interrupt her, so he sat patiently as he waited for her to continue.

"I like you," she said, finally. "I really do. But I want to be very clear that I have no intention of staying here long term. I might not know if I want to continue acting, but that doesn't mean that I plan on staying in Snowy Pine Ridge. And I don't want to start something that will only end up getting both of us hurt."

The apples of her cheeks grew more and more pink as she spoke, and Clark's heart pounded in his chest. For the last three days, Valerie had been nothing but honest with him as they'd talked about everything under the sun. And he knew that it was time for him to do the same with her as well.

"I know that," he answered, nodding his head slowly. "I know that you don't plan to stay. But the truth is, before you showed up, I had resigned myself to living an unexciting life right here. No romance, no thrill. And sure, I liked it all well enough. But since you showed up, it's kind of thrown a wrench in things. And while I know that we won't last, that doesn't change the fact that you woke something up in me that I haven't felt in a really long time. So I'd like to see that through, if you're down. And maybe just continue getting to know each other a little bit more?"

He had to remind himself to continue to breathe as he waited for her answer, her amber eyes roving over his face. But when her lips tugged up at the corners, turning into a bright, radiant smile, relief coursed through him.

"All right," she said with a nod of her own. "Let's keep getting to know each other."

Clark smiled back at her, dipping his head to press a quick, chaste kiss to her lips before pulling away. Valerie's stomach let out a loud, angry growl, making him laugh.

"And now it sounds like we need to get you fed." Clark smirked at her. "Want to go to Frosty's with me?"

"I would love nothing more."

He grinned at her as he extended a hand, helping Valerie to her feet. When she stood, she didn't pull her hand out of his. Instead, she intertwined their fingers, giving him a soft, tentative smile as they walked hand in hand toward Clark's truck.

CHAPTER TWELVE

Shelley smiled to herself as she signed the final form for the equipment that they were renting for the showcase, making a mental note to fax them all over tomorrow. When she was done, she leaned back in her chair, taking in all the neon lights and the animated sounds that surrounded her.

She had decided to work at one of the tables in the arcade, craving the noise and the bustle over the quiet of the office. A few kids darted from machine to machine, eagerly yelling back and forth to each other as they played their games. Shelley smiled to herself, wondering when the last time was that she'd played one of the games that the rink had to offer.

Blowing out a breath, she pushed herself to standing and gathered up the papers that she'd been working on. She needed to talk to Rudolph and let him know that everything would be completed as of tomorrow. The last she had seen him, he'd been working at the snack counter, and as she turned the corner, she found him still standing there, serving up hot dogs and French fries to a group of kids.

Shelley waited behind them patiently, not wanting to interrupt. But Rudolph also didn't so much as glance her way as he began handing out the food to the children. Just as she was about to walk forward, the door to the arcade was pulled open, letting in a blast of cold air.

She glanced in that direction, and immediately had to do a double take once she realized who it was that had just walked through the door. Clark Mitchell.... And the movie star everyone had been talking about, Valerie Bernard.

The two of them weren't touching, but they shared an open, eager, and surprisingly tender smile that had Shelley immediately wondering what the two of them were up to. Clark's dark brown eyes roved over the space, and he gave Shelley a friendly wave when he spotted her.

They approached her, and Shelley didn't miss the fact that their hands brushed up against each other's as they walked. She threw a glance at

Rudolph, wondering if she should try to speak to him now or wait until after the class a little bit later.

To her surprise, the older man's face had turned pale, and he seemed to be deliberately not looking in the approaching couple's direction.

Shelley's brow furrowed, but she didn't have time to ask what was going on before Clark and Valerie were standing in front of her. Affixing a winning smile on her face, she turned toward them.

"Hey, Clark," Shelley said, beaming and pushing all thoughts of Rudolph out of her mind as her gaze swung to the woman at his side. "And you must be Valerie, rumor had it we had a movie star in town. I'm Shelley, it's a pleasure to meet you."

She extended a hand toward the other woman, who took it with a sweet smile. But just as Valerie opened her mouth to speak, people began to approach her. There were three women tittering to each other, smiling at the movie star excitedly as they clutched pieces of paper and napkins to their chest.

Valerie's eyes darted toward the women, clearly realizing that they had recognized her, before turning an apologetic smile toward Shelley.

"It's a pleasure to meet you too," Valerie said. "But could you excuse me for a second?"

She nodded as the star turned toward the

women, greeting them all affectionately as Clark and Shelley slid toward the background.

"What are you two getting into this evening?" she asked, shooting a glance over her shoulder to where Rudolph had stood just moments before. Sometime between when Valerie and Clark had entered the building, the old man had scurried away, and Shelley made a mental note to track him down later.

"I'm giving her a tour of the town," Clark explained, giving her a recap of all the places that he wanted to take Valerie.

Normally, Shelley would be over the moon about what her friend was telling her, thinking about how long she had been in Snowy Pine Ridge and that, somehow, in all that time she had never seen him quite as happy as he was in that moment. But no matter how hard she tried, she couldn't pull her mind away from her worries about Rudolph, and thinking of the way he had blanched when his gaze had landed on Valerie Bernard.

Before long, the woman in question had finished up with her adoring fans, turning back to both Shelley and Clark with a smile on her face. She apologized for the interruption, and then the three of them continued their conversation about all the things that they'd been doing so far in town.

Shelley was a bit surprised as Valerie stood talking to her, taken aback by how down-to-earth the actress seemed. With her immersion into the sports world, Shelley was no stranger to celebrities. And unfortunately, a lot of them tended to lose sight of the fact that they were humans before they were stars. And yet, Valerie Bernard seemed to be much humbler than Shelley ever would have anticipated.

As they wrapped up their conversation, Clark and his date saying they wanted to get around to playing some of the games and possibly even skating, they all said goodbye. The moment the duo turned away from Shelley, she darted down the hallway that led to Rudolph's office. She stood for a moment outside the door, listening to make sure that he was inside before she heard the tell-tale sign of his fingers tapping against the keyboard keys.

She knocked once but didn't wait for his response before barging through the door. The old man's head shot up from where he sat behind the desk, his eyes narrowing on Shelley instantly.

"What's going on?" she demanded before he had time to try to kick her out. She placed her hands on her hips, staring him down. "Why have you been in such a mood lately?"

"I don't know what you mean," Rudolph grumbled, his gaze dropping to his desk as he fidgeted absentmindedly with the papers on it.

"Yes, you do," Shelley said forcefully, not letting him dodge her inquiry. "You ran away the moment you laid eyes on that woman. So tell me, what is going on?"

"Movie stars are just silly," he answered, voice still low and grumbly while he refused to meet her eyes. "It's all so frivolous and people like that tend to be shallow. So I didn't want to interact with her. Which is my business."

He turned his gaze back to Shelley, his eyes still narrowed as he inclined his head toward the door behind her.

"And I don't appreciate you barging in here and demanding answers that you have no right to. So, if you don't mind, I have work to do. Make sure the door is closed on your way out."

He looked back at his computer, beginning to type slowly as he picked up on his work. Shelley paused for only a moment, wondering if she should push the issue before deciding against it. With a shake of her head, she turned and strode out of the office, closing the door like he had asked.

She had no idea what was going on with Rudolph, and he could claim it was related to whatever perceived frivolity he had surrounding movie stars if he wanted to, but she knew better. The one thing she now knew for certain was that whatever was causing the older man's foul mood, it had something to do with Valerie's arrival in town.

And Shelley was going to do whatever she could to figure out exactly what it was that he had against the actress.

* * *

"I never expected you to be that terrible at pinball." Valerie laughed as she and Clark walked hand in hand through town.

They had stayed in the arcade for a couple hours, bouncing from game to game as they challenged each other and laughed with glee as one or the other won. But now, they were walking toward Valerie's hotel while the cold air nipped at both of their noses.

"I'm not bad at pinball," Clark argued, squeezing her hand. "You're just ridiculously good at it."

He brought her hand up to his mouth, kissing the back of it before his brow furrowed with worry.

"Your hand is freezing," he observed, opening his mouth to blow hot air across the back of her palm. "Did you not bring any gloves?"

Valerie shook her head. "I forgot."

"Well, my house isn't very far, it's on the way to the hotel. Do you want to stop there for some tea and to get warm? Then I can take you home in my truck whenever you're ready?"

Valerie smiled at him. "That sounds lovely."

The two of them continued along their path as delicate snowflakes began to fall around them, turning the town into a sleepy little snow globe, and it wasn't long before Clark, still holding onto Valerie's hand, turned off the sidewalk and began walking up toward a small, white house.

It was cute, and quaint in a way that Valerie hadn't anticipated. She waited patiently as he took his keys out of his pocket and unlocked the door before letting her inside. Immediately the warmth wrapped around her, making the bits of her skin that had been exposed to the cold of the outdoors sting a bit with relief.

"I'll put some tea on," he said, kicking his snowy

boots off at the door. "The living room is right through there, feel free to make yourself at home."

She smiled at him before turning and walking in the direction that he had indicated. Valerie tried as hard as she could not to be nosy as she walked toward the living room, but her curiosity ended up getting the better of her. And the moment she stepped into the living room, she began looking at the pictures on the wall, all of them depicting people that looked so much like Clark that they had to be the rest of his family.

She could hear him clinking around in the kitchen as she moved away from the walls toward the plush sofa in the center of the room and plopped down onto it. And just as she was about to settle back into the overstuffed cushions, something on the coffee table caught her eye.

Valerie sat forward, hand darting out to grab the DVD case just as Clark entered, carrying two steaming mugs of tea.

"I thought you hadn't seen any of my movies?" she asked, grinning as she held the case up for him to see.

"I hadn't," he explained, plopping down next to her, and handing her one of the cups. "But I thought it was time that I changed that. I watched about half of it earlier before I had to leave to meet up with you."

He paused for a moment, and Valerie watched as his face turned hesitant and slightly embarrassed.

"Do you want to finish it with me?" he asked, his voice unsure.

She pursed her lips, amused by the idea. "Are you sure?"

He nodded, and Valerie couldn't stop her answering smile.

"All right," she answered, bringing the warm mug up to her mouth and taking a sip, allowing the steaming liquid to heat her up from the inside out. "I actually haven't seen this movie since the premiere years ago. So it'll be nice to watch it again."

Clark's answering grin lit up his face as he picked up the remote and switched the TV on, getting everything ready and then pressing play on the movie. They both settled back into the couch, and not even five minutes had passed before Clark threw his arm around her shoulders and allowed her to snuggle into his body.

Valerie leaned her head on his shoulder, relishing in how good it felt to be that close to him.

"You're an incredible actress, you know that?" Clark mused, his voice filled with awe.

She was glad that he wasn't looking at her, not as she felt her cheeks flush with joy.

"Thank you," Valerie murmured.

She had been complimented on her acting skills plenty of times in the past, but for some reason Clark's words seemed to hold more weight than anyone else's ever had. She felt it when he shifted next to her, turning his body so that he could glance down at her. Slowly, his hand came up to her chin, tilting it up so that they could meet each other's eyes.

And as if in slow motion, Clark bent down to kiss her. Valerie couldn't stop herself from leaning into the kiss, from allowing it to heat her all the way to her very soul.

Just like the first time they had kissed, Valerie knew that it was likely a bad idea. She had no plans to stay in Snowy Pine Ridge, and part of her suspected that she was just setting herself up for heartbreak. But she couldn't pull away from Clark. Not when the feel of his lips against hers felt so good and so right.

So she let the kiss continue, assuring herself that if she was going to hurt her own feelings, then at the very least, she could make sure that she took advantage of every second before the fall.

CHAPTER THIRTEEN

"Dad, you're going to break your neck," Clark called, climbing out of his truck. He pushed the door shut and then strode across the yard toward where his father was struggling to hang the Christmas lights.

"You mind your business, son," his father grunted, but he didn't protest further as Clark steadied the ladder.

He stood below his father, who was reaching to one side to hang a string of lights as he hung on to the ladder with one hand. Clark gripped the metal ladder tightly as his father finished the strand he was working on, and as soon as it was safe to do so, his father climbed up onto the roof. Clark quickly followed behind him, eager to help.

"Is that Clark I hear?" His mother's voice floated

up from the yard, and the two men paused to look down as she came into view.

Maureen and Kenneth Mitchell, Clark's parents, had been high school sweethearts. And after so many years together, they knew absolutely everything about each other, and loved nothing more than some good-natured prodding at each other.

"I'm sure he was about to hurt himself," Maureen called up. "Thank you for helping him. I'm sure he hasn't said it yet."

She smiled affectionately at her husband, just as Kenneth grunted, "I was getting to it!" Clark couldn't help but laugh at his parents, happy to see that nothing had changed since he had been around for dinner the week prior.

He and his father made quick work of the rest of the decorations, working in tandem easily as they had for Clark's entire life. When they were finished, they climbed back down the ladder and admired their handiwork.

"In a bit of a competition with the neighbors," Kenneth admitted, dipping his head to indicate the house to the right. "But don't tell your mother."

Clark laughed and mimed locking his lips as they both turned and headed into his childhood home. The moment he stepped through the doorway, the familiar scent of the home enveloped him, and he inhaled it deeply.

"Dinner is coming out of the oven now," Maureen called the moment she heard the door snap shut behind the two Mitchell men. "Go ahead and get settled at the table."

Clark and his father did as they were asked, pausing only long enough to take off their coats and to kick off their boots at the door. Both of them knew that his mother would have their hides if they tracked snow through the house.

They settled into their usual spots and Maureen placed the food in the center of the table before they all began to serve themselves. They chatted while they ate, and Clark was glad to see that she'd made one of his favorites—meatloaf with garlic mashed potatoes. His parents filled him in on everything that had been going on since he saw them during their last, weekly family dinner. And then, once they had finished, they both looked at Clark expectantly.

He cleared his throat, taking a moment to gather his thoughts before he shared what he wanted to tell them.

"So, I do have some news," he said, his voice shaking slightly with nerves. "I started seeing someone."

His mother let out a small gasp of excitement while his father beamed.

"Well, that's great to hear," Kenneth said with a grin.

"It's still new," Clark said hastily, not wanting them to get the wrong idea. "We're still figuring things out and getting to know each other. But I just wanted to let you know before anyone else in town spilled the beans."

Maureen nodded, and he could tell that she wanted to ask more but was restraining herself. It was moments like this that Clark wished he had a sibling, someone at family dinners that he could count on to take a bit of the focus off him. But thankfully, his mother seemed to pick up on the fact that he didn't want to say any more.

"Well, if you're happy, then we're happy. Isn't that right, Kenneth?" she asked, shooting her husband a pointed glance so that he immediately grunted his agreement.

There was a brief pause where the three of them continued to eat their meals, and then his mother attempted to change the subject.

"Did you hear that there's a movie star in town?" she asked, looking at her husband and her son with obvious excitement.

One of the reasons that Clark had decided to not tell his mother who he was seeing was because he knew she was a fan. He wanted to give her time to get used to the idea of him even seeing someone before telling her exactly who it was. And he had to fight back a smile as he thought of just how much she would freak out if he told her just how familiar with the movie star he was.

"I heard that!" his father chimed in. "Heard she's been traipsing all over town getting to know the locals. Everyone speaks real highly of her."

"Isn't that something?" Maureen said wistfully, shaking her head with a far-off look in her eyes. "Valerie Bernard in Snowy Pine Ridge. Maybe if I get lucky, I'll get to meet her."

Clark couldn't hide his grin, so he glanced down at his plate, unable to stop himself from thinking that if *he* was lucky, his mother would absolutely be meeting Valerie Bernard.

* * *

"Here we go, little Gussy," Mindy cooed to her pup as she put his final leg through the hole of the coat she was wrestling him into. "It's time to go outside!"

The furry little dog twirled excitedly around her

feet, yapping joyfully as she hooked his leash to his collar and then opened her front door. Gus bounded down the stairs in front of her, making sure to keep just close enough so that his leash wasn't too taught as he trotted into the snow. And Mindy couldn't help but notice that he was prancing and showing off in his new, bright blue coat.

She looked down at her own body, at the matching coat she'd bought for herself and grinned. The two of them walked through the snow-covered streets of Snowy Pine Ridge, with Gus stopping to sniff every few feet. As they walked, people from the town stopped to say hello to them, and it filled Mindy with a sense of warmth and belonging.

Since arriving a year ago, she had finally felt like she'd found her place in the town. People liked her and liked her business, and especially they liked the way that she and Sarah collaborated to bring them deals between their two bakeries. And Mindy had never lived in a place that felt more like home.

Which made it all the more important for her to finally pick the perfect show-stopping dessert for the upcoming Christmas showcase. Now that Baking Fiend was decorated, and she and Sarah had worked out all of the kinks with the collaborating deals that they'd be offering, her mind was drawing a blank on the creativity front. It had been days that she'd been tossing around idea after idea, and none of them seemed to stick.

Gus barked, his tiny frame jumping up so that he could place his paws on one of the buildings and look in the window. Mindy walked up behind him, trying to see what had grabbed his attention, and then laughed.

In the display case were animatronic kittens riding a train. She reached down to scratch Gus's ears before they started walking again, but then something caught her eyes. Above the display window was draped greenery and sprigs of holly. The snow had accumulated on it, dancing and reflecting prisms in the twinkling Christmas lights. And suddenly, inspiration struck.

"Individual peppermint and gingerbread trifles!" she exclaimed excitedly, looking down at her dog. "I can make the layers look like the snow and how it sparkles over the town. Oh, Gus! You're a genius."

She darted forward, scooping the enthusiastic pup into her arms and holding him to her chest as she walked quickly back toward the bakery, wanting to make a quick tester to bring her idea to life. Less than a block from the shop, she spotted a familiar face and she darted toward them.

"Well, don't you look excited?" Lacy said with a laugh as Mindy and Gus approached.

Piper, Lacy's daughter, was strapped to her mother's chest and tucked inside of her puffy down coat. Only her face was sticking out, and the child burbled happily at the woman in front of her.

"Gus here just had the best idea in the world," Mindy explained in a rush, laying out her idea to her friend. By the time Mindy was done, Lacy was grinning.

"I'm drooling just thinking about it," she said, closing her eyes as if imagining the taste. "It's going to be a hit, Mindy! I just know it. I can't wait to taste it."

"Thank you so much." Mindy beamed. "I'm going to go practice it right now."

The two women said their goodbyes before heading off in opposite directions. Mindy stopped at her house long enough to get Gus cozy all over again before heading toward the final block to the bakery, and with every step she grew more and more excited. She had to admit, with this new idea spinning in her head, it was the best that she had felt in weeks.

CHAPTER FOURTEEN

The sound of footsteps coming up onto the porch had Valerie's heart pounding in her chest, and she bounced excitedly on the tips of her toes as she turned toward Clark.

"Do you think they'll like it?" she asked, eyes wide with anticipation and he smiled at her.

"They're going to love it," he said, reaching forward to give her hand a reassuring squeeze and dropping it just as the front door was pulled open.

She, Clark, and some of the other volunteers had been at the house since early that morning, working diligently to make progress on the Hiltons' future home. And about two hours ago, Clark had received a phone call that Margaret and Stephanie were going to be swinging by just to see how things were coming along. It had warmed Valerie's heart and spurned her on to finish applying the paint to the little girl's bedroom. She had done some digging and asked around and found out that the little girl's favorite color was lilac. So Valerie had picked out the most beautiful, soft lilac that she could find to paint Stephanie's room. And now she was so nervous to find out if the child would like it or not.

The moment the two members of the Hilton family stepped through the door, their mouths dropped open in shock. Even when Valerie and Clark hadn't been at the house, other volunteers had been and the progress that had been made over the last few days had been astounding.

Almost all the drywall was done, as well as the kitchen, the windows, and the bathrooms. All that was left to do was the finishing touches like painting, the floors, and the hardware.

"This is beautiful," Margaret breathed as she stepped through the space.

"And this is really gonna be where we live, Momma?" Stephanie asked, a grin tugging across her face.

"It really is," Valerie assured the little girl and was immediately rewarded by a beaming smile.

"Stephanie," Clark chimed in, grabbing the girl's attention. "Valerie actually has something to show you."

The little girl threw a questioning look to Valerie, who just nodded.

"If that's all right with your mom," she said, looking at Margaret.

"Of course, I need to talk to Matthew anyway."

Margaret waved her daughter on before walking toward the back of the house, where Valerie knew that Matthew was working. Turning her attention to Stephanie, Valerie nodded her head toward the stairs. "This way."

Both Stephanie and Clark followed her as she led the way toward the room that she had just finished painting. The moment that it came into view, Stephanie squealed in excitement and ran forward.

"This is your room," Valerie explained, beaming as she watched the little girl's clear joy.

Stephanie began spinning around in circles, and as Valerie watched her, she felt tears prickling the corners of her eyes. Not wanting to cry in front of the young girl, she excused herself really quickly and darted down the hall toward the primary bedroom.

She didn't close the door behind her, and she

heard someone walk in just as she began to dab at her eyes to prevent the tears from falling.

"Everything all right?" Clark asked, and Valerie could hear the concern lacing his tone.

She nodded before turning around to face him. "It's all happy tears," she explained. "It's just overwhelming. And it's putting things into perspective."

"That's good though, right?"

He took a step toward her, reaching out his arms, and she gladly threw herself into them.

They stood there like that, locked in an embrace for a long moment as Valerie basked in the comfort of his arms.

"It's just making me realize that I've been so focused and wrapped up in my movie career that I forgot to pay attention to everything else," she admitted, finding it much easier to open up now that her face was pressed snugly against Clark's broad, warm chest. "And I love acting, I do. But the constant focus on my age, and the dog-eat-dog world of it all, it just has me feeling a bit disenchanted by it all. And then, being here, in this town and with all of you, it's making me realize what it's like to be fulfilled by other things too."

She felt his chest move as he took a big, deep breath before expelling it, and she wrapped her arms around him even tighter.

"I know it's selfish of me to say this," Clark began. "But I'm really going to miss you when you leave."

"I know," she said with a nod. "But even when I go home, it doesn't mean we have to lose touch. Because the truth is, I don't want to give this up. Not when everything about you and this place helps me feel so grounded."

She moved back a bit, giving them just enough distance that she could look up at his face without stepping out of the comfort of his arms. Clark was looking down at her, a broad smile curving his lips.

"I'm fine with keeping in touch if you are," he said with a wink, making her chuckle.

Slowly, Valerie's spirits began to lift, and as Clark reached up a hand to wipe away the final remaining tear that was clinging to her cheek, Valerie found herself leaning into his touch.

She wasn't sure what her future would bring, but in this moment, here with this man, she felt happier and more fulfilled than she had in years.

***

Shelley sputtered, reaching forward to take a swig of the water in front of her to wash the horrendous taste out of her mouth as Sarah did the same beside her.

"What was that?" she croaked, turning to glare at William, who was trying to bite back a laugh.

"It's awful, is what it is." Sarah made a face, throwing a horrified look in her fiancé's direction as she too tried to cleanse her tongue of whatever it was that they had just drunk.

"It was muddled juniper berry, espresso, and eggnog. I thought it would be good!" William argued, his cheeks flushed with embarrassment despite his still grinning face.

"Do *not* put that on the menu," Sarah said forcefully. "If you do, we will never have another customer for the rest of our lives."

William laughed and agreed before turning around and beginning to work on his next concoction while Sarah iced a few cupcakes and waited for her next batch of cookies to finish. Shelley had arrived about an hour earlier, wanting to bounce some ideas off of her two friends for how to drum up excitement in surrounding towns to get more business for the showcase.

Meanwhile, William had decided that it was the perfect time to try out some new holiday drink recipes and have both Sarah and Shelley try them out. Shelley had to admit that some of them had been quite good. But unfortunately for her taste buds, most of them had not.

"I know that everyone in town is excited," Shelley explained, taking another big drink of water to try to banish the lingering taste of juniper berries. "But I don't know if word has traveled even one town over. We'll have tourists, just because it's that time of year. But I was hoping to get people coming in just for the showcase."

"We could make flyers!" Sarah proposed, moving her piping bag with a flourish as she put the final swoop of icing on the Santa Claus cupcakes she was putting on display.

"But what would we put on them? Just the fact that there is a festival?" Shelley asked, trying to envision doing that in a way that makes it enticing.

"I mean, people know that we throw amazing holiday events," Sarah said, placing the cupcakes in the display case one by one. "I'm sure they'll come no matter what."

"Here," William interrupted, turning around and extending a small taster cup to both women with a flourish. "A new one!"

Shelley eyed it warily and then brought it up to

her nose to give it a delicate sniff. This one, at least, smelled better than the last one. She brought it to her lips and a delicious, sweet flavor exploded across her tongue.

"Now this one is a winner!" Sarah said, smiling at her fiancé as Shelley nodded her agreement.

William beamed at them, proud of himself as he turned to begin working on another thing for them to taste. The timer on the oven went off, chiming through the small space loudly as Sarah excused herself to go and retrieve the cookies. She returned a few moments later, carrying the hot tray and setting them on one of the cooling racks.

"I was hoping Valerie would come in," she explained, shooting a look at the cookies. "I've been keeping gingersnaps in stock ever since she mentioned they're her favorite. Don't want our movie star to go without."

At the mention of the celebrity's name, Shelley perked up.

"That's it!" she exclaimed, snapping her fingers as an idea began to take place. "We have Valerie Bernard!"

Both William and Sarah shot her confused glances and Shelley shook her head.

"We can talk to her about potentially getting the word out about the showcase! We can theme the night around one of her movies, and we can have her act as a quasi-spokesperson. More people are bound to show up if they think they're going to meet a movie star," Shelley exclaimed, filled with excitement over the idea.

"I don't know," Sarah put in with a quick shake of her head. "I've been around Valerie a few times, and I think she wants to remain as anonymous as possible while she's here."

Shelley nodded, feeling a bit like the air had been let out of her balloon. "That's fair, but it doesn't hurt to ask, right?"

She watched her friends as the couple shared a look, some wordless conversation that she wasn't privy to passing between them. After a brief pause, Sarah turned her gaze back to Shelley and gave her a soft, encouraging smile.

"It doesn't hurt to ask," she confirmed, making Shelley perk up all over again. "If you'd like, I can ask her if she wants to have a girls' night one night? We could propose the idea to her then? And then just let her know if she doesn't want to be involved, well, that's entirely okay."

"This is going to work," Shelley said, nodding vigorously as a grin plastered itself across her face. "I just know it will."

CHAPTER FIFTEEN

Valerie walked up to the wrought iron gate, peering toward the door of the house to see if it was, in fact, the correct one. She glanced down once again at her phone, at the GPS she had used to walk here using the address Sarah had given her the day before, and sure enough it said that she'd arrived. But the houses in this part of town were so closely packed that she was certain it would have said that for possibly all of the houses right in the area she was standing.

Thankfully, the door was pulled open at that moment, and a smiling Sarah was waving her in. Valerie rushed forward, not wanting to spend any longer in the cold than she needed to. She might have fallen a bit in love with the town, but she hadn't gotten entirely used to the weather just yet.

"Valerie's here, everyone!" Sarah yelled as soon as the door was shut behind them.

A chorus rose up from deeper in the house of, "Hey, Valerie," "Hi, Valerie," and "We're back here." She turned her attention to Sarah.

"Who all came tonight?" she asked, a bit nervous that this was going to end up being a much bigger to-do than had been indicated during the invitation.

"Well, come and see," Sarah said with a grin before turning and walking ahead of Valerie through the cozily decorated but a bit cramped hallway, her blonde ponytail swishing merrily behind her.

Valerie just nodded, even though the other woman couldn't see her and followed after with a gulp. The noise of everyone talking got louder as she followed Sarah, and the next thing she knew they were stepping through a doorway into a cozily decorated kitchen.

She exhaled an immediate sigh of relief when she saw only three other women at the table, much fewer than the noise had made it seem like. She recognized most of the women—obviously there was Sarah, Mindy from Baking Fiend, Shelley from the arcade, and then another woman whom Valerie didn't know.

That woman had honey brown hair with hints of

red in it, and green eyes that were so vivid and expressive it was a bit startling. She was also grinning like mad at Valerie.

"Hi," the woman Valerie didn't know said as she pushed herself up from her chair and extended her hand. "I'm Lacy. I believe you met my husband, Derek."

"Ah!" Valerie made a noise of recognition, recalling her run-in at the hardware store with the man in question and how he'd mentioned that his wife was a fan. "Yes! He told me about you, and Clark mentioned you a few times as well. It's a pleasure to meet you!"

Both Valerie and Sarah sat down at the table at the two remaining seats, and Valerie leaned forward to sniff at the dishes in the center of it. A heaping bowl of spaghetti and meatballs, a giant Italian salad, and a pile of breadsticks decorated it, and the smell of it all made Valerie's mouth water.

Now that they were all there, they began piling their plates high with food, the women chatting amongst themselves, and Valerie was pleased to find how easy it all was. They didn't treat her like she was different, which, unfortunately happened to her all too much.

"You know," Lacy said around a giant bite of

meatball, looking at all the other women around her with wide eyed excitement. "This is the first bit of time I've had away from Piper since she's been born."

"Mommy's gone wild," Sarah said with a waggle of her brows, lifting the glass to her lips with a grin and making the other women laugh.

"I don't know about all of that." Lacy chuckled before turning her eyes back to Valerie. "So you said Clark told you about me. Have you two been spending a lot of time together?"

Valerie blushed, looking down at her plate and taking a few bites before answering.

"A bit," she admitted sheepishly, and all the other women at the table shared a long look.

"They definitely came into the rink the other day together." Shelley was grinning from ear to ear.

Every eye turned toward Valerie and, somehow, her blush got even worse.

"I like him," she admitted, knowing that she wouldn't be able to hide the truth. "More than I planned to, honestly. But it's all so complicated."

"How so?" Lacy asked, cocking her head to the side in question.

Valerie didn't even stop to contemplate it as she spilled it all out. She told the women about her time with Clark, and about the role her agent found for her. She talked to them openly and honestly about her worries about going back to Hollywood, about how no matter what she did she felt like she'd just be living on borrowed time. And how in such a short amount of time, Snowy Pine Ridge had already made such an impact on her that it had her doubting everything she'd ever known.

Silence filled the small kitchen when she finished, until Sarah reached across the table and placed her hand on Valerie's, giving it a soft squeeze.

"You already feel like a part of our community," Sarah said softly, a kind smile lighting her face. "And we might be biased, but Clark is a good man. We support whatever you want to do."

"But we would be lying if we didn't tell you we wanted you to stay," Mindy chimed in, her corkscrew curls bobbing as she gave an emphatic nod.

"Which brings us to another thing," Shelley added, almost sheepishly.

Valerie noticed Sarah giving the other woman a quick look, but Shelley didn't tear her eyes away from Valerie.

"I know you've heard about the showcase coming up," Shelley continued on, her voice soft and coaxing. "We were thinking that it might drum up a little more interest if we theme some things after one of your movies. Specifically, the ice-skating showcase, and tying it to the movie *Love in Bloom*. It fits in really well with the decorations and choreography we already have."

"And you won't have to do much at all," Sarah said quickly, giving her a reassuring smile. "Your involvement can be kept minimal. And you can say no at any time."

"Okay," Valerie said with a nod, surprised and honored that they had even thought of her. "I'm in."

And just like that the other women were beaming at her. They finished their dinner before all making their way to the living room. They surprised Valerie with some of her own movies to choose from, and she picked out her favorite.

They all curled up on the large sectional, but none of them could stop talking long enough to actually watch the movie. Slowly but surely, the night devolved into a good old-fashioned sleepover. And when Lacy asked Valerie about the special effects makeup in *Love in Bloom* that had made her look like an old woman, the makeup boxes got brought out and they all began practicing 'old age makeup' on each other, pulling up videos on YouTube to double check their technique as they went.

Valerie felt almost giddy as she swiped her brush over Mindy's face, giving her deep smile lines. She couldn't remember the last time her heart had felt quite this light.

Clark closed the door of his truck as he walked around to the bed of it, taking careful steps to not slip on the snow and ice in Shelley's driveway. Earlier that day, some of the items that she'd needed for the showcase had been dropped off, and despite the late hour, he still wanted to bring them over and drop them off.

He loaded up his arms, holding everything steady as he made his way to the front door. As he got closer, he heard the telltale sound of laughter floating out of the house and he couldn't help but peer through the living room window.

It took him a moment to make sense of the sight before him, because at first all he saw was a group of old ladies cackling around the fire. But then, he caught sight of one of them with familiar bangs and honey-colored eyes and started chuckling and shaking his head at how well the women had done on their makeup.

He lifted his fist and rapped it against the door, hearing an excited squawk from inside. There was a bit of bickering about whether or not they should answer, but soon he heard the deadbolt unlock and the door was pulled open.

"Clark!" Shelley yelled loudly, clearly announcing who was at the door to the other women in the house. "What a surprise!"

"Some of your stuff came in for the showcase," he said, shifting the stuff he was holding in his arms. "Wanted to bring it by."

"Absolutely, come inside."

Shelley stepped to the side, waving him through the door and Clark stepped through the threshold. More yelling sounded from the living room as he walked into it, with a few of them ducking behind pillows.

"Looking good, ladies," Clark told them with a chuckle as he set everything down in the corner Shelley indicated.

His eyes landed on Valerie, and he felt his cheeks grow hot with a blush.

"Do you want any cookies or tea? I made some fresh ones this afternoon." Shelley asked, grabbing Clark's attention once more.

"I'd actually love a cookie," he answered.

"Hey, Valerie," Shelley said, a grin lighting her face as she turned to glance at the other woman. "Want to take Clark to get a cookie? They're on a plate in the kitchen."

He tried not to roll his eyes at Shelley's blatant setup, but he didn't fully succeed as he laughed at her. Not that he was going to argue with it, he'd love a bit of alone time with Valerie.

Clearly embarrassed at the callout but also not wanting to say no, Valerie pushed herself to her feet, gave Clark a soft smile, and then walked past him toward the kitchen. Just as he turned his back, he heard Lacy, Mindy, Sarah, and Shelley all tittering to each other about the "budding new couple."

It was a bittersweet feeling—watching Valerie get so close to everyone here and fitting in so seamlessly and knowing that she wasn't going to be staying.

"Here you go," Valerie said as they reached the kitchen, walking immediately over to the plate of cookies.

She plucked one delicately off the top and took a big bite, smiling up at him as she reached out her arms in a request for a hug. Eagerly Clark pulled her toward him, holding her close to his body before kissing her softly on the forehead.

"You're a cute old lady," he murmured into her hair, and he felt her shoulders shake as she laughed.

When they parted, he watched as Valerie used the sleeve of her sweater to wipe at her face, but all it did was smear the makeup further. He chuckled, reaching up to help clean away the dark smudges of her mascara.

"I'm glad you're fitting in with everyone," he said, nodding his head toward the living room where they could still hear the other women tittering amongst themselves.

"I am too," she answered, and he could hear a bit of melancholy in her voice, and he wondered if she was thinking the same thing he had been.

"I want you to know," Clark murmured, his voice low and sincere, "that no matter what happens when you go, having this time to get to know you better has made this the best Christmas season I've had in a very long time."

Valerie blushed so hard that her cheeks turned a rosy pink.

He lifted her chin and brought his lips to hers, hoping that she could feel the truth of what he'd said in their kiss.

CHAPTER SIXTEEN

Shelley blew out a shaky breath before bringing up her fist to knock on the door to Rudolph's office. She'd known that she needed to talk to him about the showcase all day, but her nerves continued to get the better of her and she kept putting it off. But there was no more time to stall, not when she also needed to tell him about the minor changes it would cause for the setup in the showcase.

"Yeah," Rudolph grunted from inside, prompting Shelley to push open the door.

The old man glanced up at her, his face set in its typical scowl as he asked, "What?"

"I have an update about the showcase," Shelley said, trying her best to keep her voice from shaking. She had figured out enough to know that Valerie was a trigger for the old man, for whatever reason. But surely, he'd be able to see the benefit in having a movie star tied to their event? Or at least, that was what she hoped.

"Go on, spit it out."

She walked farther into the office, taking one of the seats across from Rudolph.

"A few of us were talking and we wanted to drum up a little more interest in the surrounding towns," she explained carefully. "And we figured what better way to do that than to get Valerie involved, so we asked her if we could theme the ice-skating showcase..."

She didn't even get a chance to finish her sentence as Rudolph pushed himself away from the desk and began shaking his head.

"No," he demanded. "Absolutely not."

"Why not?" Shelley argued back. "Surely you know that it's only a good thing if people from all around come to see us. And Valerie can help with that."

"This town can stand on its own," Rudolph insisted. "We don't need movie stars coming in here and stirring it all up."

"Rudolph, please," she began, her eyes tracking

him as he walked quickly around the desk toward the door.

"No."

That was Rudolph's only answer as he stormed out of the office, slamming the door behind him. Shelley stayed seated, not sure how things had gone so incredibly wrong. She had assumed that he wouldn't be thrilled with the information, but she hadn't anticipated a flat-out refusal.

"Why does he seem to dislike this woman so much?" Shelley said to herself, shaking her head as she contemplated it.

She racked her brain, thinking of everything that she knew about Valerie from reading magazines and news articles over the years, but nothing that Shelley could remember would warrant such a reaction from Rudolph. She stood, walking toward the door, and pulling it open. She half expected the old man to be on the other side, rearing and ready to give her a piece of his mind about including Valerie. But of course, the hallway was empty.

She pulled out her phone as she walked, making her way to the rink, pulling up Google and immediately typing in Valerie Bernard. The first result that popped up was a wiki page dedicated to the actress, and Shelley clicked on it. She read through it quickly, eyes skimming for anything of particular interest.

"Landed her first big movie role at the age of nineteen," she murmured to herself. "Moved to LA when she was eighteen, did some commercial work before that. Did theater in high school and was raised by a single mother named Paula... wait."

Shelley blinked as the picture she'd seen of Rudolph with some mystery woman flitted through her mind suddenly. That woman's name had been Paula, and Shelley had thought that she'd looked familiar. Now that she considered it more closely, she realized it was because the woman vaguely resembled Valerie.

Quickly, she searched 'Valerie Bernard's mother.' Immediately, images filled the screen and she let out a small gasp. The woman in the photo had for sure been Valerie's mother. She and Rudolph had known each other!

Going back to the original article, she began skimming it again. Looking for anything additional about Valerie's mom. But there weren't any more mentions of her, apart from the fact that she had passed away not too long ago. There was, however, a mention of the fact that her father had never been in the picture, and as far as anyone knew, the man's identity was unknown.

"Oh," Shelley whispered, her hand fluttering to her mouth in shock. "Oh my."

Puzzle pieces began fitting themselves together in Shelley's mind, forming one question and one question only. Was it possible that Valerie was Rudolph's daughter?

* * *

Valerie stepped back, whipping the back of her hand across her brow to clear it from the sweat as she studied the wall she'd been painting. It was a beautiful, sage accent wall that she'd picked out after talking to Margaret and found out about her favorite colors. Valerie had arrived at the house about an hour before, wanting to make headway before Clark showed up. She couldn't help but want to make him proud of her.

Her phone began ringing, a bright cheery noise, and the suddenness of it made her jump. Valerie bent, setting down the brush so that it wouldn't drip onto the floor, and then walked over to the windowsill she'd set the device in. Glancing down at the screen, she let out a small groan before reaching down and pressing 'accept.'

"Hi, Florence," she said immediately, pressing the phone to her ear.

"Valerie, darling," Florence said excitedly, speaking so quickly that her words blended together. "I have the best news, the absolute best. Are you ready for it?"

Wanting to get the conversation over as quickly as possible, she nodded. "Yup, go for it."

"*Lose You to Love Me* has been nominated for a Heart Award!" Florence crowed, and Valerie could hear her jumping up and down and clapping on the other end of the line, clearly having put Valerie on speaker.

"A Heart Award? Really?" She couldn't keep the surprise from leaking into her voice.

That was one of the most prestigious awards for romance movies out there. There had been plenty of her movies that had been nominated in the past, and they'd even won one for the best screenplay. But she had kind of expected that portion of her career to be over.

"Yes. And what's better, not just the movie is nominated. But *you* were nominated! For best actress!"

Florence continued chattering away on the other end of the line, telling her all about how this might be the thing she needed to save her career, how the offers would be flying in after this. But Valerie didn't have it in her to listen.

Her heart was swelling with pride, there was no doubt about it. This was something she had always dreamed of. But she wasn't as elated as she imagined herself being. It was clear from the way that Florence was talking that she wanted her back in L.A sooner rather than later, especially since there would be press associated with the nomination, but Valerie just couldn't give her an answer. Not yet.

"Listen, Flo," she said, deliberately using the name she knew Florence hated so that her agent wouldn't be tempted to keep talking. "I'm so sorry, but I'm working on something at the moment. I'll call you back later, okay?"

She didn't give Florence time to respond as she disconnected the call. Valerie felt awful about it, but she couldn't think about that all now. Her mind was reeling in a thousand different directions.

"Hey," came a voice from behind her, and Valerie whirled to see Clark standing in the doorway holding a beautiful bouquet of flowers.

Her stomach erupted in butterflies, and a huge smile tugged itself across her cheeks.

"Those for me?" she asked, nodding toward the flowers.

"These things?" he asked, shaking the bouquet before shaking his head with a sly grin. "Nah, I ran into Rudolph Hutchins on the way over and he confessed his undying love for me."

She laughed, remembering vaguely the stories that she'd heard about the old man from the people in town. She thought she had seen him while she'd been at the arcade, but he had disappeared before she could be introduced.

"Well, looks like I have competition then," she muttered, her grin widening as he closed the distance between them, kissing her gently.

When they broke apart, he handed her the bouquet of flowers and she sniffed them, giving him time to look around the room she'd been working on.

"This looks great," he said, letting out a low whistle as he turned on the spot.

"I would have been a little farther along, but I got interrupted by a phone call."

He must have noticed the change in her voice when she mentioned the call, because he whirled to face her, brows furrowed.

"Everything all right?"

She blew out a breath. "Yeah. No. Maybe."

Valerie began filling him in on everything, telling him about the award and how this was everything she'd ever wanted, but now she wasn't so sure. When she finished talking, Clark walked forward and wrapped her in a hug.

"I support whatever decision you want to make," he said. "And I'm here if you want to talk."

She nodded, her cheek brushing against the fabric of his shirt, but still her mind was racing. Los Angeles and acting was all she had ever known. There had never been a time in her life where Valerie had considered doing or being anything else. But all she did know was that no matter what she was going to take every moment with Clark that she could get, because she wasn't ready for their time to end. Not yet.

CHAPTER SEVENTEEN

Clark grunted with effort as he lifted a box of supplies, placing it on a shelf for later use. All day he'd been lost in thoughts of Valerie, thinking of how much he liked her, how much everyone seemed to like her. And how terrible it would be for everyone involved when she finally left.

A bell chimed out in the store, and he immediately placed it as the one above the door, announcing the arrival of a customer. He took a minute to dust himself off, especially after spending most of the day in the storage room, and then strode out into the shop.

Derek was standing in the doorway, Piper strapped to his chest with only her head peeking out between the zipper of his jacket. His friend broke out in a grin the second his eyes landed on Clark.

"Hey there," Derek said, walking toward him. "Thought I'd bring in this ol' gal to see you. Was just down in the kennels with the dogs and Lacy, and then Piper started to get fussy."

Derek reached up, ruffling the one-year-old's head beneath the knitted toboggan she was wearing. Piper giggled excitedly, and Clark could see her feet kicking from underneath Derek's down coat.

"I hear babies will do that from time to time," Clark joked, approaching the two with a smile.

When Clark stopped in front of them, he bent down so that he was at eye level with the little girl. He puffed out his cheeks and crossed his eyes, making a silly face that elicited an excited shriek from her.

"How are things going? Seems like she's doing better." Clark stood, walking over to the counter, and leaning on it.

"She's doing a lot better," Derek answered, following after him with Piper babbling happily. "But she has decided that it is a lot more fun to throw her baby food instead of actually eating it. Lacy got hit directly in the eye by pea puree today."

Clark laughed at the image, seeing Lacy in his

mind's eye with mushy, green paste splattered across his face. But then, the image in his head started to shift, and suddenly it wasn't Lacy's face he was seeing in his mind—but Valerie.

He could see it all. The way she would look as she smiled at a baby, one that looked a lot like her... and a lot like Clark.

Clark shook his head quickly, banishing the thought from his head and eliciting a curious look from his friend.

"I heard you stopped in to see Valerie at girls' night the other night," Derek said, raising an eyebrow and Clark wondered if his friend had been able to read his mind.

"I stopped in to give Shelley stuff for the showcase," Clark corrected. "I actually didn't know she was going to be there. But seeing Valerie was an added bonus."

"Likely story."

"And a true one," Clark said with a chuckle.

"Did you hear that she's going to be involved with the showcase?" Derek asked, prompting Clark to nod.

"She told me."

"It's good that she's fitting in with everyone." Derek looked down at his daughter, not meeting his friend's eyes. "It's going to be tough on the town when she leaves."

Clark felt the words all the way in his stomach, the thought of her leaving making his nerves feel like they were being tied in knots.

"It is," he admitted, and then launched into a brief explanation of what Valerie had told him. The offer for the new movie, the award nomination, it all spilled out about it.

Until Clark started talking about it, he hadn't realized just how devastated he was going to be when Valerie headed back home to Los Angeles. And it felt good to get it off his chest.

The image of Valerie with the baby pervaded his mind again, and he tried to push it down. But this time it refused to leave. This was the first time in his life that Clark had been able to picture a future like that with anyone. And it was a shame that the first time it was happening was with the one person that it would likely never come to fruition with.

He told Derek as much, his heart pounding as he admitted that he could see a future with Valerie. Derek's brown eyes went wide with surprise, and then softened into something like pity when the reality of what that meant hit him.

"I won't stand in her way," Clark said earnestly,

still whole heartedly meaning everything he had said to Valerie about supporting her the other day. "When she goes back to her life, I'll support her with everything I have. I'll be happy for her, even if I'll be sad for me."

"That can't be an easy situation," Derek responded, shaking his head slightly at his friend's turmoil. "And it's really noble of you to support her. But have you talked to her honestly about how you feel yet?"

Clark shook his head. "No. I don't want to put that burden on her. I don't want her to feel like she has to stay for me."

"But do you think that she can make an informed decision without all of the information?"

Derek was staring at him, his eyes slightly pinched at the corners with obvious concern for his friend. Clark's heart gave a twinge of gratitude for the care that Derek was showing him.

"She deserves to know," Derek continued, speaking softly. "And you deserve to know that if she does decide to go home, she made that decision knowing every possible option that there was. Neither of you deserve to always be wondering 'what if.'"

Clark nodded, hearing the sense in what Derek

was saying. But that didn't stop how terrified the thought of confessing it all to Valerie made him feel. He knew there was a possibility that he might bare his heart to her, lay it all out and tell her how he felt, and then she'd take those feelings and his heart and leave.

"No risk," Derek said pointedly, "no reward."

Clark laughed, thinking about the slogan that they used to tell each other in high school before their football games. They'd always tell it to each other before they went against their coaches wishes, calling out a play that they knew was risky but that could end up winning them the game.

In his heart, Clark knew that Derek was right. There was no way he could deny it.

But now the question was—how would he find the courage to do it?

* * *

The rink was silent, not a soul in sight other than Shelley and Rudolph as they finished up cleaning everything down after the practice for the showcase. The question she'd posed to herself the other day had plagued her nonstop, and now the possibility of it all threatened to overwhelm her.

Steeling her spine, she walked hastily toward where the man in question was working behind the counter, disinfecting and putting away the skates that had been used earlier in the day.

"Rudolph," she said as she approached, positioning herself so that she was standing in front of the opening that led behind the counter. "We need to talk."

"Busy," he grunted, keeping his eyes focused on the pair of skates in his hands.

"I saw the picture," Shelley blurted. "I know the truth. I know about Paula."

His hands stopped moving as his knuckles tightened on the skates he held. Slowly, his gaze moved up to meet hers before his eyes narrowed.

"What do you think you know?" he asked, his voice hesitant and loaded with skepticism.

"I know that she was Valerie's mother. And I know that you had some kind of romantic thing going back in the day."

"Worked that all out for yourself, did you?" he murmured, placing the skates on their shelves and trying to move out from behind the counter, but of course finding Shelley barring his way.

"I'm not moving until you finally talk to me about this," Shelley told him, making sure that he heard how serious she was in her tone. "You've been in a horrible mood ever since Valerie arrived in Snowy Pine Ridge, and I think I know why."

"Oh, you know why, do you? By all means, enlighten me."

"I think you're Valerie's father."

Rudolph's spine straightened as the words fell between the two of them. And then, the old man did something that Shelley hadn't expected in the slightest. He threw his head back, and he laughed.

"You think... I'm her... *father?*" he repeated between guffaws, and Shelley just stared at him, waiting for him to get himself under control.

Slowly, his laughter petered out, with Rudolph swiping at his eyes to clear them of tears that had sprung up in the midst of his mirth.

"All right, Shelley," he said, humor still dancing in his eyes. "You're not wrong that this woman's presence has thrown things off for me. I'll admit that, especially since you aren't really giving me a choice. But I hate to tell you that with the rest of it, you're barking up the wrong tree."

"So you weren't romantically involved with Paula Bernard?"

Rudolph's cheeks flushed. "I didn't say that."

A silence filled the air between them, and

Rudolph began shifting nervously from foot to foot. He seemed to be waging some internal battle, and Shelley ventured a guess that he was trying to figure out exactly how much he wanted to tell her.

"If I move, are you going to go running toward your office?" Shelley asked. "Or would you go sit down with me in one of the booths and we can actually talk?"

Rudolph chewed the inside of his cheek, before shaking his head. "I won't run. We can talk."

Relief flooded through Shelley at his words as she stepped aside, allowing the old man to stride past her. She half expected him to take off toward his office anyway, but he didn't. Instead, he stayed true to his word and strode toward the nearest booth, sliding into one of the seats and waiting patiently for Shelley to do the same.

When she did, he looked down at his hands where they rested on the table, studying them for a moment before he glanced up at her.

"I'm not Valerie's father," Rudolph began, a faraway look in his dark brown eyes. "But I was in love with her mother."

"How did you two meet?" Shelley probed.

"She came to Snowy Pine Ridge, years and years ago. We met while she was here and it was a whirlwind. We had an instant connection. She was one of the loveliest people I ever met, inside and out."

He grew quiet for a moment, seeming lost in his memories.

"She was here for several months, and I thought she might decide to stay," he continued. "When she first came to Snowy Pine Ridge, she was estranged from her family, but they reached out to her and reconnected at some point. I was happy for her, glad she had that family connection back, but then they started putting pressure on her to return home for good."

"I'm assuming she did?" Shelley asked, and Rudolph nodded.

"She did. Eventually. It was a few more months, but I could tell that her heart wasn't here anymore. She missed Montana, missed her family, and ever since they'd started talking to her more, they'd also started getting in her ears about me."

Shelley's eyebrows shot up. "What about you?"

Rudolph shrugged. "Wasn't good enough for her, I guess. Her family was well-to-do. And they had someone picked out for her to marry. Not an arranged marriage, per se. But close to it. And she didn't want to disappoint them."

"So she went home?"

He gave her another nod. "She did. She went home and she married him. I hated it, but what can you do? Turns out he was horrible to her. Word traveled to me about the divorce, through some of her friends that she'd introduced me to while she was visiting."

Shelley's heart gave a pang of sympathy for the old man as he shook his head.

"By the time I found out about it," Rudolph explained, "I felt like too much time had passed. I thought about it, about going out to Montana and telling her that I wanted her back. Would have raised that baby girl like she was my own. But I was a coward. And the more time that passed, the more impossible it felt to reach out."

She nodded. "I can't imagine how difficult it all was."

She watched as Rudolph's throat bobbed, and she could only imagine the barrage of emotions that were coursing through him at that moment.

"I followed her career," he murmured as he stared somewhere off into the distance, speaking low enough that for a moment, Shelley wondered if he was so caught up in his memories that he was talking to himself. "Valerie's. Did you know that?"

His eyes flicked back to Shelley, and she shook her head.

"I did. Saw her on a magazine once and she looked so much like her mother, I knew instantly who she was. Didn't even need to read the title or her name. Kept up with her all these years. And then when I heard about Paula's passing."

His voice choked off, and Shelley couldn't stop herself from reaching across the table to where his hands rested on the table and taking one, giving it a reassuring squeeze. Rudolph looked at it, clearly surprised by the sympathetic gesture, but he didn't pull away.

"I am so, so sorry," Shelley began, speaking as softly as she could. "Have you thought about telling Valerie any of this?"

Immediately, he shook his head. "I can't put all of this on her. She's just a girl."

Shelley snorted. "She's thirty. And maybe, she might want to know. I mean, she lost her mom. Her dad is clearly out of the picture. It might help her to have some kind of connection to family. Even if it's just because you both loved the same person."

Rudolph was silent, his gaze turning pensive all over again and she could tell that he was mulling it over.

"At least think about it?" she asked, tilting her head to the side.

She allowed him a few moments to remain silent, not wanting to pressure him into a decision he wasn't ready to make, but also not wanting him to push the idea to the side either.

"I'll think about it," he finally said, the corner of his mouth ticking up into a small, hesitant smile.

Shelley squeezed his hand again before letting go, bringing her arm back to her side of the table and giving him a smile of her own. She wasn't sure if Rudolph would decide to approach Valerie and at the very least talk to the daughter of the woman that he'd loved. But she really hoped that he did.

CHAPTER EIGHTEEN

Valerie ran her fingers through her hair to smooth down any fly-away pieces a second before she climbed out of the old cab in front of The Rustic Hearth. It was another restaurant in town, one that sat a little bit removed from Main Street, and it had an upscale feel to it that Valerie hadn't been expecting based on the name.

She thanked the man who had driven her there before climbing out of the car and walking across the parking lot. Clark had offered to pick her up, but she'd declined. She had wanted a bit of extra time to think before arriving at the date.

Valerie still didn't know where they stood. Whether they were casual or how they were supposed to be behaving. She knew that it could never amount to much, not when she still intended to leave. But then again, the more time she spent in Snowy Pine Ridge, the more she considered if maybe staying was what she wanted.

She pulled open the door and walked into the threshold, immediately getting wrapped up in the warmth and the atmosphere of the place. Gunmetal sconces and chandeliers dotted the space, complementing the dark wood walls and the rich burgundy fabric of the rugs and the tablecloths. And the smell of the food drifting out to her from the kitchens was heavenly.

Valerie walked up to the hostess, giving her Clark's name, and was immediately escorted through the restaurant toward a table. Clark was already there, and when he glanced up and saw her, he rose from his seat and hustled to the other side of the table to pull out her chair.

He hugged her in greeting, pressing a kiss to her cheek before the two of them settled into their seats.

"You look beautiful," he told her, eyes shining with so much sincerity that it made Valerie blush.

"And you look very handsome," she replied, giving him a soft smile.

Immediately, they launched into conversation, catching each other up on their days and then talking about how things were going at the Hilton house. And happiness exploded through her when he advised that they'd be able to start moving in the following day.

They were interrupted briefly by the waiter coming to take their order. She ordered the spaghetti and black truffle meatballs, while Clark ordered a steak. Valerie watched him as the waiter walked away, not able to stop her thoughts from drifting to how grateful she was for the man in front of her.

"What are you grinning about?" he asked as the waiter walked away, noticing the look on her face.

"You," she answered, her smile widening as she said it. "You're always so... steady."

He cocked his head to the side. "What is that supposed to mean?"

She chuckled. "It's a good thing. It's just everything about you is so good and so sure. Pulling my chair out for me when I came here, you hold the door open everywhere we go, how kindly you treat everyone around you. What you're doing for the Hiltons. All of it."

Clark shrugged, his brown hair glinting in the soft light of the restaurant. "It's just the way I was raised."

Valerie considered that, trying to picture the

parents that had created a man like Clark. The idea alone made her want to meet them. But before she could embarrass herself and blurt that out, she clamped down on the thought, harkening back to what she'd been stewing over earlier in the cab.

She still wasn't sure if she was staying. And she felt like it would be unfair to bring up meeting his parents if they were going to be going their separate ways in a few short weeks.

"What are you thinking about?" Clark asked, and Valerie scrambled to come up with a believable lie.

Thankfully, she was saved by the return of the waiter and the arrival of their food. They dug in, and she moaned at the taste.

"The food is so good here," she said around a bite of meatball. "Back home, everything is so *healthy*. Which, don't get me wrong, I like that too. But there, everyone is always so terrified to gain even a pound that everything is leeched of so much flavor. It's all raw carrot juice or a kale salad. And then there's this."

She took another bite of the meatball, groaning again and Clark laughed, shaking his head.

"I genuinely don't know how you do it," he said,

grinning at her after a bite of his steak. "I would die if I lived out west."

"After living here your whole life, I can kind of see why," she answered honestly, grinning at him.

Valerie didn't miss the way his eyes flared at her words, his thoughts written plainly on his face. She could see the way that hope flared so clearly within him when she talked about loving this place, hoping that she'd stay. But Valerie just wasn't sure if she could do it, if she could leave everything she'd ever known and live in Snowy Pine Ridge. She didn't want to get his hopes up just to smash them if she ended up leaving anyway.

Clark would never say anything about it, and she knew he would never pressure her or make her feel like the decision was anything other than entirely her own. But that didn't stop her from feeling guilty when she saw such raw hope lingering in his handsome face.

She was spared having to say anything else when the sound of Clark's name was being muttered across the restaurant.

They both turned, and immediately, her gaze landed on a man that she didn't know, although she recalled having seen him at the rink. He gave them both a wave, approaching the table with his hands stuffed in his pockets.

"Hey, Rudolph." Clark gave him a welcoming grin. "What are you on this side of town for?"

"Picking up a bit of dinner," he replied. "Just waiting for them to bring it out. Thought I'd come over and introduce myself since I was busy when you all came into the rink the other day."

He turned to Valerie, and she couldn't help but notice the way he was blushing.

"I'm Rudolph Hutchins," he said.

She expected him to extend a hand for her to shake, but he didn't. He just stood there a bit awkwardly, looking at her with an expectant look on his face.

"My name is Valerie Bernard," she said, giving him what she hoped was an encouraging smile. "It's nice to meet you."

His eyes roved over her face, a bit like he was studying it and trying to commit it to memory, the way someone would a loved one. Valerie tried not to squirm. One of the staff members approached, carrying a to-go bag, and extending it to Rudolph.

"All right, then," the older man muttered. "That was all. I'll be going now."

Clark and Valerie said goodbye to him, then sat

in silence while they watched the man walk out the door.

"That was strange," Clark muttered. "Rudolph is usually so prickly that it's like pulling teeth to get him to talk to you, let alone approach someone while they're having dinner." He turned to Valerie, a smirk tugging up the corner of his lips. "Maybe he's a secret romance movie fan."

She rolled her eyes at him, waving away his words. "Or maybe he just felt bad for being busy the other day."

"Well, whatever the reason, now you've officially met Rudolph Hutchins. Because what small town would be complete without their own grumpy older resident?"

Valerie chuckled. "Is he really that bad?"

Clark shook his head. "No, he's harmless. Just don't take it personally if the next time you see him, he's a bit crotchety. He's like that sometimes and tends to not like many people. So if he's grouchy—just know that everyone else loves you."

She laughed, shaking her head at this new piece of information. There was something about the old man that she thought seemed familiar, but she couldn't quite put her finger on it. Valerie turned back to her spaghetti and dug back in, returning her attention to Clark as he began filling her in on the latest antics of Derek and Lacy's daughter, Piper.

Before long, all thoughts of Rudolph Hutchins and his strange familiarity were driven entirely out of her mind.

* * *

Clark grinned at Valerie from the doorway of the Hilton house the following day, watching with interest as she made her way over the snow-covered driveway toward him. The moment she was within arm's reach he swooped her into a hug, brushing a brief, enthusiastic kiss to her lips.

"I can't believe it's today," she gushed excitedly, prompting him to chuckle.

"I know," he said, watching as she pranced around the main floor, taking it all in. "Derek and Matthew wanted to be here for it. But Derek has a sled tour and Matthew has a house showing. So it's us!"

"I'm kind of glad," she said softly. "Don't get me wrong, the guys are great. But I want a moment to say goodbye to the house."

He chuckled. "Say goodbye to the house?"

"Uh-huh." She nodded, grinning from ear to ear. "I learned a lot here!"

"True, you looked like a half-drowned kitten when you showed up here the first day, and now look at you."

"Hey!" she yelled, giving him a joking punch to the arm as she smiled up at him.

Clark didn't say it, but he was happy they had the house to themselves for a moment too. Especially as he pulled her to him and kissed her again. Thoughts of his conversation with Derek pushed themselves into his brain, of how his friends had told him that while supporting Valerie was great, it might also be worth it to let her know how he felt.

And as he looked down into her beautiful, open face, he couldn't hold it back anymore.

"I need you to know something," he said in a soft, almost reverent tone. "I need you to know that I support whatever decision you make when it comes to staying or going. Don't get me wrong, it'll suck to say goodbye to you. But if that's what you choose, I'll support you. But if you stay, I'd support that too. And if you did... I'd be open to more if you were."

The words fell into the space between them, Valerie's eyes dancing as she studied his face.

"I don't want you to think I'm pressuring you,"

he continued, adamant that she knew he would never want to force her hand. "But I just wanted you to know that if you stayed, you wouldn't be alone."

She opened her mouth, taking a breath as she began to respond. But the moment the very first syllable started to leave her lips, the door was thrown wide open, and the Hilton children began pouring in.

Stephanie was whooping loudly, running around the bottom floor with her hands over her head as her brother and sister filed in hesitantly. Matthew was behind them, grinning as he found Clark and Valerie in the house.

"I thought you had an open house," Valerie said as the man approached, smiling at him, and Clark couldn't help but notice her expression was stilted. The warmth of the smile not entirely reaching her eyes.

"I was able to have someone take over for me. I wanted to be here for this, and then I ran into them on the way over," Matthew explained, beaming around at everyone in the house.

The noise carried on as Margaret and Jeff, her husband, walked through the place, everyone murmuring happily as they took it all in. Clark felt proud of the work that he, Valerie, and everyone else had done here. Especially as the Hiltons gushed about how much they loved their new home.

But no matter how hard he tried, Clark couldn't shake the nagging worry in the back of his mind over what Valerie had been about to say.

CHAPTER NINETEEN

"No, no, no," Mindy said on repeat as she shifted the cardboard box back and forth in her hands.

She'd placed an order for adorable, champagne flutes that she was going to use for the individual trifles. And they'd been delivered earlier that afternoon. She'd placed them in her office, telling herself that she'd get them out and clean them after the bakery closed for the day. Of course, once she'd opened the box, she realized that almost every single flute that she ordered had been either chipped or completely shattered.

Immediately she pulled out her phone, dialing Landon's number as she started to pace. He answered on the second ring, and the noise of the background let her know that he had something else going on.

"Hey, babe," he said as the call fully connected, sounding as aloof as always. "What's going on?"

"Landon, it's awful!" she admonished, feeling pinpricks of tears at the corners of her eyes. She felt silly for wanting to cry over something like this, but she'd had a vision of how everything would be for the showcase, and it felt like that vision wasn't going to happen now. "All of my champagne flutes that I ordered for the showcase are broken. I ordered them just for this because I wanted them to be a non-standard size, and now even if they mail me replacements they won't be here in time. And.."

"Are you upset because some glasses are broken?" he asked, interrupting her in the middle of her sentence. His tone wasn't unkind, necessarily. But it also wasn't as attentive as Mindy would have hoped.

"Yes! The ones that I ordered for the trifles I was telling you about."

The sound of yelling in the background amped up, and she could hear him cover up the phone and say something to whoever he was with. He returned a moment later, and she could hear that he was laughing.

"Listen, babe, can't you just buy new glasses? It's not a big deal, it'll all be fine, and your truffles will be perfect."

"Trifles," she corrected. "And I know..."

"I'm so sorry," he said as another round of yelling filled her ears. "I know you're upset. But I'm kind of in the middle of something. I've gotta go. I'll call you later. And I promise, Min, it'll all be fine."

He didn't even wait for her to say goodbye before he disconnected the call, and Mindy was left standing in the middle of her empty bakery staring down at the phone in her hands. Embarrassment unfurled within her, and the tears that she had felt earlier began to fall. Her phone began ringing, and for a moment she thought it would be Landon, calling to apologize. But when she looked back at the screen, she saw it was Sarah that was calling.

"Hello," Mindy sniffed, trying her best to hide the fact that she was crying, but clearly failing at it because the moment the word left her lips Sarah began speaking in a rush.

"Oh my gosh, Mindy, are you okay? Are you crying? What happened?"

Relieved to at least have someone to vent to, Mindy began telling her everything. The champagne flutes, Landon's dismissal, and how what originally had just been a minor, frustrating inconvenience now felt insurmountable.

"I'm so sorry," Sarah said in a soothing voice. "I can't believe Landon didn't at least hear you out. But I do have good news, at least. I made individual strawberry shortcakes in champagne flutes a couple years ago. And I saved all of them. I have them in storage here at Sweet Thing. I can bring them to you if you want."

Mindy's spirit lifted at that, smiling despite the tears still glistening in her lashes. "Are you serious?"

"Absolutely. I'm almost done at the bakery for the evening, and I can bring them over in probably fifteen minutes?"

"I'll be here! Sarah, you're a lifesaver," Mindy breathed gratefully.

They said their goodbyes and then Mindy hung up the phone. Thinking about how glad she was that her friend had been able to come through for her. Sarah's willingness to hear her out and to jump in and help threw a stark and unflattering light over her conversation with Landon.

Mindy was still finding it hard to believe that he hadn't listened to her, that he hadn't been able to walk outside or to somewhere he could hear her for only a few minutes, just to let her vent about her frustrations over what had happened.

She had to admit that he'd been absent for a while now. And while things had been great when they had first gotten together, they had become complacent rather quickly. And she wasn't entirely sure she liked the way things were anymore.

Before she could overthink it, Mindy pressed a few buttons on her phone and brought it to her ear. When Landon answered again, the background noise was a little bit quieter, letting her know there had been a less noisy place when she'd called earlier, he just hadn't been willing to go to it.

"Hey, Min," he said. "I know you're upset. But can I call you back later, I…"

"I'm sorry, but I need to talk now," she said in a rush. Her tone was high pitched with her nerves, and she tried as hard as she could to get it under control.

She and Landon may have their problems, but he wasn't a bad man. He just wasn't the right one for her, and she didn't want to leave him feeling hurt.

"I don't think this is working out between us," Mindy said, much calmer this time, her voice soft as she continued. "We're both so busy, and we haven't been able to make time for each other. And I think you know as well as I do that neither of our hearts are in this."

There was a pause where the only thing that filled her speaker was the sound of whatever restaurant or bar Landon was in.

"You're breaking up with me?" he asked, and Mindy was happy to hear there was no malice or hurt in his voice, just a bit of confusion and what she could have sworn was relief.

"I am," she said as kindly as she could. "And I think we both know it's for the best."

Landon blew out a breath, and she could almost see him beginning to pace back and forth and running his fingers through his hair.

"All right, then, yeah," he finally replied. "I guess this is goodbye then. Take care of yourself, Min."

"You too."

She hung up the phone and set it on the counter. Standing in the middle of her empty bakery, she expected to feel sad. And she was. But not in the sense that she had expected.

She wasn't sad that she was no longer with Landon. She had meant what she said to him and could admit now that they'd both just been going through the motions. But she was sad that it meant she was going to have to start from scratch again.

Thankfully, there was a knock at the bakery door just then, distracting her before she could start worrying about having to date again. She glanced at the door, seeing Sarah and Will on the other side of it.

Each one was holding a large box that she assumed was filled with the champagne flutes. Mindy walked to the door to let her friends in, and the moment they entered they set the boxes down.

Sarah turned to her, eyeing her up and down.

"What else happened?" she asked, and Mindy had to fight the urge to blanch.

"How do you know anything happened?" Mindy fired back, prompting William to shake his head.

"She has a sense about these things," he said with a chuckle. "It's best to just tell her. But do it after I go."

"You're going already?" Mindy asked and he nodded.

"I was just the muscle to carry the boxes." He turned, giving Sarah a kiss and waving goodbye to Mindy before walking out the door.

Sarah, however, didn't spare any time. The moment that the door had closed, she whirled on her friend.

"Spill," she demanded, walking over to one of the stools at the counter and plopping onto it.

Mindy came to sit beside her friend on one of the stools, telling her all about the breakup. And as she spoke, she knew for a fact that it was the right choice. Especially when the more she spoke, the more relieved Sarah seemed.

She knew that getting back out in the dating world was going to be hard, especially when she was always surrounded by so many strong, amazing couples. But the truth was, she wasn't going to find her William, her Zach, or her Derek by staying in a relationship where she was just going through the emotions. And even if it was scary, Mindy was also excited.

Because how could it go wrong when she had friends this great to see her through it?

CHAPTER TWENTY

The door to the rink was pulled open, grabbing Shelley's attention as she was putting the final touches on a piece of tinsel that had been arranged to look like a flower. She whirled to face the sound of the noise, and immediately her face broke into a wide, excited smile as Valerie strode through the doors.

She looked beautiful and stylish in well-fitting black jeans, a black sweater, and black booties, and she was grinning at Shelley as she approached. It was the night of the showcase, and Shelley was so excited she could hardly sit still. She kept rearranging and fixing the already perfect decorations.

"How are you?" Valerie asked as she stopped at

the edge of the rink, and Shelley trotted over to her to pull her into a quick hug.

"Nervous," Shelley admitted with a chuckle, shaking her head a bit.

"That's to be expected."

Both of them glanced at the clock, seeing the amount of time left before people began arriving. The kids would begin showing up in about an hour, and about thirty minutes after that, doors would be opening for the showcase.

"We've been preparing for this showcase for so long," Shelley said. "It's hard to believe that the day is finally here."

"It's going to be great," Valerie reassured her. "Do you want to go over the plan one more time?"

Shelley nodded, launching into the timeline of how everything would break down. Once the doors opened for people to take their seats, the kids would be escorted to the back to the locker rooms, and precisely at three p.m. they would skate out and begin their performance. During the intermission, Valerie would come out and thank everyone for coming and give a small speech about Snowy Pine Ridge and what attracted her to the town, and then the rest of the showcase would commence.

Valerie nodded, confirming that she understood

the game plan. Then, Shelley noticed she placed her hands in the pockets of her jeans, beginning to shift her weight nervously from foot to foot.

"Can I talk to you about something?" Valerie blurted, her eyes wide and hesitant before shaking her head. "Sorry. I just don't have a ton of people I trust back home. All of the friendships I've made are just kind of surface level, and you seem so close with all the girls and I...."

Shelley held up her hands, smiling at the other woman as she was getting herself worked up.

"Hey. Hey, it's okay," she said softly. "You can talk to me about whatever you need to."

"Are you sure?" Valerie's eyebrows drew together, and she looked so concerned that Shelley's heart gave a squeeze of sympathy.

"Of course," she answered, nodding her head with encouragement. "Talk to me about whatever you want."

Valerie gave her a grateful smile. "It's about Clark," she said, and then began filling Shelley in on everything that Clark had said to her while waiting for the Hiltons to come to their new home.

The longer Valerie talked, the more Shelley's heart ached for the other woman. She had no idea what this must feel like for her, to feel as if she was caught between giving up everything that she had ever known and giving up the possibility of true love.

"What do you think you're going to do?" Shelley asked after Valerie finished filling her in, and the other woman shook her head.

"I have no idea," she answered honestly. "I mean, it's crazy, right? Thinking of uprooting my entire life and moving to an entirely different state just because I met a guy. That's the kind of stuff that only happens...."

"In movies?" Shelley asked, raising her eyebrow, and giving Valerie a pointed look.

The actress blushed. "Well, yeah. Who hears about this kind of stuff happening in real life?"

Shelley laughed, shaking her head. "It happens more often than you'd think. Just talk to everyone around town. Snowy Pine Ridge is magic, and it tends to bring people together in the strangest ways."

"I really like him, Shelley," she admitted, worry clouding her light brown eyes.

"I can tell that you do. And he likes you too. That's clear enough. And the beautiful thing is that you don't have to decide right now. You aren't leaving tomorrow. There's still time."

Valerie nodded, her eyes turning pensive, and Shelley was sure she was turning over all her options in her mind. Movement at the far side of the rink caught her eye, and she spotted Rudolph coming out of his office.

He'd told her yesterday that he'd talked to Valerie the other night, but he hadn't given her much detail. Shelley got the urge to ask Valerie about it, to see if anything happened that was actually worth mentioning. But she figured that if it had been noteworthy, she would have heard more about it by now.

Rudolph Hutchins tended to play things close to the chest, but she couldn't imagine him not telling her the full story if he'd come clean about his past relationship to Valerie's mother. He still hadn't told her if he planned to give Valerie the full truth or not, despite the fact that Shelley had made it vehemently clear that she thought he should.

The door to the rink was pulled open, letting a blast of frigid air to blow through as the first kid that would be performing in the showcase arrived. It was an eight-year-old girl named Candace, and her eyes went wide the moment they landed on Valerie.

"Looks like we're on," Shelley said, giving the other woman a wink.

She noticed that Valerie still looked hesitant, her gaze distant and clouded, and her brows creased with worry for the woman Shelley now considered a friend.

"Hey," she said gently, low enough so that Candace wouldn't overhear as she snapped Valerie out of her own thoughts. "It's all going to work out exactly like it's intended to. And while I may not be able to tell you what to do, I can tell you that you can trust yourself to make the right decision for yourself. Take the time you need, weigh your options, and listen to your heart. That's all you can do."

Valerie's eyes clouded over with something that resembled gratitude before shaking her head as if to clear her emotions away.

"Thank you," she whispered, just as she turned to face Candace who was approaching shyly, plastering a beaming smile on her face. "And who might you be?"

Just like that, Shelley and Valerie were caught up in a whirlwind of kids showing up, parents asking questions, and final preparations for the showcase. Shelley wished that she had more time to talk to Valerie, but it would have to wait until after the showcase. She just hoped that nothing too crazy would happen before then.

* * *

Valerie stood at the edge of the rink, watching as the small bodies of the skaters zoomed around the ice in perfect succession. She was in awe of their grace, especially when all of them were still at such a young age. The oldest kid in the showcase that evening was fifteen, and she was finding it quite hard to believe that anyone could possess that much talent so young —let alone enough children to pull off an entire performance.

She glanced behind her, seeing Rudolph Hutchins standing only a few feet away, absorbed as he watched the kids perform. She'd tried talking to him earlier, asking if he was excited for the show and if he'd had any hand in training and choreographing the routines, but he'd barely grunted out a response, shifting awkwardly on his feet before all but running away to work the concession stand.

Valerie had wondered if somehow, in the brief interaction they'd had at the restaurant, she'd done something to offend him. But she didn't see how that could be true. Not when she'd only spoken a handful of words to him at most.

She recalled Clark's words about the man, telling her that he was often very grumpy and to not take anything too personally when it came to him. And, while Valerie might be used to some of the shadiness and cattiness that took place in Hollywood, for some reason what was happening with Rudolph felt a bit more personal. She just couldn't put her finger on why.

The performance on the ice ended, and then Shelley skated out, holding a microphone high while she began the intermission. Valerie's own heart was beating wildly as she waited for her cue to walk out, going over the short speech she had prepared over and over again. She didn't know why, but she found herself more nervous for this than she ever had been for anything else, including award shows, talk shows, and huge auditions.

"...and with all of that in mind," Shelley called out, her voice ringing out loud and clear through the speakers that were scattered around the space. "Please give a massive round of applause for none other than Valerie Bernard, star of the movie *Love in Bloom*, which our showcase tonight was inspired by!"

Valerie took one final, quick breath before walking out onto the ice. They'd talked briefly about having her skate out onto the ice, but she hadn't been able to get the hang of it. So she walked delicately to the center as she heard Rudolph readying the Zamboni for when she was done.

"Thank you, Shelley," Valerie said, taking the

mic from her friend as she reached the center of the ice and then looking out at the crowd. "And thank you, Snowy Pine Ridge, for your huge welcome and your hospitality during my stay here!"

She scanned the seats as she talked, eyes almost immediately finding Clark who was sitting front and center. Her heart skipped a beat at the sight of him beaming at her from behind the protective glass, and she felt a swell of joy as she continued with her speech.

She had practiced for hours the night before, going over it again and again until she got it just right. It was no different than reciting lines, and all those years of honing her acting skills came into play now.

She talked about Snowy Pine Ridge, and why she chose here as her place of retreat, weaving in the story of her mother and how she used to tell her about the magic of the town, especially at Christmastime. Valerie talked about how, as she grew older and her mother grew sick and would still talk about this place, about the love she had for it and for the people here, she began to think that maybe time had caused her mother's memory to make it too fantastical, because the way her mother described it was too perfect to be believed. But then, she got here, and it turned out, her mother had been right.

By the time she ended her speech, tears were pricking at the corners of her eyes as she thought of her mother and of the memories she made here. The crowd stood, giving her a standing ovation as she thanked them and then handed the microphone back to Shelley.

Valerie turned and strode toward the back of the rink again, seeing Rudolph perched on the Zamboni just beyond the wall. The man's face was red and his expression unreadable as she got closer to him. But he was definitely refusing to so much as look at her.

For some reason, it made Valerie feel embarrassed as she walked past him, taking up her previous spot along the back wall as Shelley wrapped up and Rudolph drove onto the ice. Valerie didn't know what she had done wrong, but it was clear that she'd done something. And she made a promise to herself to go find the man and make things right with him as soon as she could.

"You did amazing!"

A voice floated to her from a few feet away, snapping her out of her confusion about Rudolph. Valerie's head snapped up, finding Clark standing there with a large smile and an even larger bouquet of roses and a teddy bear.

She stood, wrapping her arms around him and pulling him into a tight hug as he kissed her forehead.

"Thank you so much for being here," she whispered, letting herself relax for a moment in his embrace.

His arms tightened around her, and she reveled in his warmth, soaking it up to help give her strength.

"I wouldn't have missed this for the world," he said, his deep voice rumbling where her cheek was pressed to his chest.

"Still, it means more than you could know."

He leaned down and kissed her, sending her stomach into a freefall just as the Zamboni trundled its way back toward them, the ice now smooth, glistening, and ready for the next performance. Valerie's eyes tracked the movement of the massive machine and the man on top of it, before glancing back up at Clark.

"I'll come out and watch the rest of the show with you from the seats in just a sec. Is that okay?"

A confused look fluttered across his handsome face, but he didn't pepper her with questions. Instead, he just nodded before kissing her on the forehead once more and then walking back toward his seat. The moment Clark was out of view, she set the flowers and bear down by her bag and walked in the direction that Rudolph had disappeared in.

Valerie found him just as he was turning the machine off and climbing off of it. The old man must have heard her approach, because as soon as she rounded the corner his eyes were on her.

"Sorry," he grunted a little awkwardly, his eyes darting down to the ground instead of at her. "But I'm a bit..."

"I'm sorry for whatever I did to you," Valerie blurted, not meaning to cut him off but not wanting him to run off before she was able to apologize.

"What?" he asked, his dark brows knitting together as he cocked his head slightly.

Valerie let out a shaky breath. "I've noticed a bit of tension between us today, and I'm not entirely sure why. So I just wanted to say I'm sorry if I did something to offend you. I can't say that I recall doing anything, but whatever it was, I assure you I..."

"It's not that." Rudolph was shaking his head.

The old man blew out a breath before walking over to lean against the nearby wall. He seemed to be struggling to find his words, and Valerie kept her distance as he took the time he needed to consider what he would say.

"I knew your mother," he said after what felt like an eternity. "Paula. I knew her. I loved her. I..."

His voice broke, and Valerie watched as he reached into his pocket with a shaking hand, pulling out a picture and extending it to her. Her mind was reeling as she walked forward and took it, finding it to be a picture of a handsome young man with his arm slung over the shoulder of a much younger version of her mother.

"I don't understand," she said, shaking her head as she glanced from the picture to the man in front of her and back again.

So Rudolph began to explain. As more details about his love story with her mother came pouring out of him, her head started to ache. And by the time he finished, Valerie found that she didn't know what to say. She felt overwhelmed with the information, and she needed a moment to process.

She glanced back at Rudolph and found that he was wearing an expression that matched her own, and she knew that neither of them were exactly ready to finish the conversation.

"Thank you for telling me," Valerie said, finding

her voice thick and raspy with emotion. "I just... I think I need a minute."

She extended the picture back to him, and Rudolph took it, folding it back lovingly into his pocket as he nodded. He didn't say anything else as Valerie turned and walked away, feeling more awkward than she ever had in her life as she made her way toward Clark.

The moment he saw her he knew that something was wrong, and he gave her a concerned look. Valerie could tell he wanted to ask her about it, but she just shook her head.

"Later," she promised as she took the seat next to him.

Clark nodded and they both turned their attention toward the rink, where the next group of kids were coming out to take their positions.

Later, she promised herself. She'd think about it all later. And Valerie allowed herself to get distracted by the performance in front of her, and the steady warmth of the man at her side.

CHAPTER TWENTY-ONE

Clark shot off a text to Valerie before stuffing his phone back in his pocket as he walked out of Sweet Thing Bakery with a coffee in hand. He had wanted to spend a little more time with her the night before, after the showcase, but she'd been distracted and claimed she wanted to go back to her hotel room. Her texts had been a bit short and distant ever since, and it had Clark feeling a little worried.

Almost as soon as he dropped his phone in his pocket, it buzzed with a new text, and he had to fish it out all over again. He opened the response from Valerie and smiled. He'd asked if she wanted to meet up, and she said yes. She was at the town square looking at the Christmas tree and invited him to meet her.

"See?" he muttered to himself as he began walking quickly toward where he'd indicated in her text. "Told you everything was going to be all right."

But Clark realized he had spoken too soon as he stepped into the town square and spotted Valerie. She had the same look on her face that she'd had the night before. Worry coursed through him all over again.

A halfhearted smile tugged at her lips as she caught sight of him, waving at him to join her on the bench in front of the tree.

As Clark plopped down beside her, he offered her a sip of his coffee and she accepted it, leaning her head on his shoulder as they both sat and stared at the tree.

"Rudolph Hutchins was in love with my mother," Valerie said with a sigh, and shock coursed through Clark as the words settled in.

"What?" he asked, dumbfounded by the news as he made sense of what had been said.

"He told me last night at the rink," she explained, the same far-off note to her voice as she spoke. "She came to Snowy Pine Ridge years before I was born. Stayed here for a while it seems. They met and fell in love, then she came back to California to marry my dad."

He felt her shrug one shoulder as if it was all no big deal, despite the strange tone of her voice.

"How are you feeling about all of that?" Clark asked, turning his head so that he could look down at her where her head still rested on his shoulder.

"I don't know," she answered honestly. "I've been trying to wrap my head around it ever since I found out. My mom was devastated when my dad left. I might have been young, but I remember enough of it. And she struggled with being a single mother so, so much. Then, when she got sick, I could tell she got even lonelier. I did everything I could, but it wasn't enough."

She took her head off his shoulder, turning her body on the bench so that she was facing him, and Clark did the same. His heart hurt for her as he looked at the worry and concern on her face, hating that she was feeling like this.

"I can't help but think if maybe she would have been better off, if *we* would have been better off if he'd come and found her."

Clark nodded, not able to argue with that logic. Especially not when the thought seemed to be hurting her so much.

"I can't imagine how hard that was for the both of you," he said honestly. "But there's also a possibility that he didn't know, not in enough time to actually do anything about it. Or maybe he did know and he was terrified. There could be a thousand reasons for him not finding her."

"I know," she said simply. "And whatever his reasoning, I'm not mad at him at all. You know what they say about hindsight. But I still can't stop thinking about how different things could have been."

Clark nodded. "I think that's normal. Considering every what-if after a big revelation like this is always natural. Do you want to talk to him about it?"

"I do," she admitted. "Because regardless, we both loved the same person. I don't want to feel so alone in this, and I want to know his side of things. But I think I just need a minute to get my head around it."

"Also normal," Clark said, looking down at her.

She seemed to have perked up a bit now that she'd gotten it all off her chest, and she gave him a soft smile.

"Thank you," Valerie murmured, leaning up to brush her lips against his before settling back against the bench.

"For what?"

"Just allowing me to vent."

He shrugged one shoulder. "Any time."

She let out a breath. "Well, I appreciate it. It helps."

Clark gulped nervously before grinning at her, hoping that what he was about to do went exactly as planned.

"I don't have to be in the store today," he told her. "One of my employees is running everything. Do you want to go back to my place and watch a movie? I can cook, or we can order food. Whatever you want."

"Will there be coffee?" she asked, looking greedily at his coffee cup that he still held in his hand.

Clark laughed, handing the to-go mug to her and allowing her to drink deeply from it.

"There will be whatever you want," he answered, still chuckling as she handed the coffee back to him.

"Then I'm in."

She beamed at him, and he stood to help her to her feet. With his hand wrapped around hers, they walked through town, heading toward his house. He was glad she said yes to going back with him. He knew his time with Valerie was beginning to dwindle. She still hadn't brought up what he'd said to her at the Hilton house, and he wasn't going to pressure her. Especially not now with all the information that she was trying to process.

He would allow himself to feel sad about her impending departure on another day. For now, he was perfectly content to spend the remainder of the day with her, and to try to make her feel better by whatever means necessary.

CHAPTER TWENTY-TWO

Valerie and Clark made the short walk back to his house in less than ten minutes. Thankfully, the air wasn't as cold as it had been, and the walk, while still rather brisk, didn't have her nose stinging by the time they made it indoors.

Clark walked in front of her as they made their way through the door, which was strange because he always held doors open for her. She didn't think too much into it as she crossed the threshold into the house, and she didn't look around as she kicked off her snowy boots and took off her jacket at the door. But the very moment she walked a little farther down the entryway, stepping around the small corner that led to Clark's living room, a loud chorus of "surprise" filled the air, and Valerie gave a small scream of shock.

In the center of his living room was a small crowd of people from Snowy Pine Ridge. Colette, Sarah, Lacy, Mindy, Shelley. They and so many more were all standing underneath a giant banner that read *CONGRATS ON YOUR NOMINATION, VALERIE.*

As everyone stood there beaming at her, Clark came up behind her, putting his hand on the small of her back as he bent to kiss her cheek.

"Everyone wanted to celebrate you the moment they heard the news," he whispered in her ear and Valerie felt suddenly overcome with emotion.

"And you organized this?" she asked under her breath, beaming at everyone else that filled the room.

"Didn't take much," he said dismissively, planting another kiss on her.

She shook her head, filled with gratitude and disbelief as she saw everyone's smiling faces. They all held up flutes of champagne, and Mindy ran forward, extending one to her.

"For you, my dear," she said with a grin, and Valerie took the drink graciously.

The Hiltons were beaming at her from in the crowd,

and her voice suddenly felt so thick with emotion that she gave a slight cough to clear it. Feeling like she had to say something, she raised her glass in the air.

"I can't tell you how much this all means to me," she began, her voice shaking with the effort of holding back her tears. "For years, I've felt out of place, like I didn't belong in the home that I created. And then when I came here, it all kind of clicked. Meeting every single one of you." She looked pointedly from person to person, landing finally at Clark. His brown eyes crinkled as he smiled at her, making her heart swell with joy as she continued. "Has changed my life in a profound, indescribable way. And I can't imagine what it's going to be like when..."

Her words died out as she realized what she had been about to say. She was going to say 'I can't imagine what it's going to be like when I head back to L.A. and am not seeing you all every day' but her mouth wouldn't form the words. They got caught behind the lump in her throat as she looked out at the people of the town who had supported her from the moment she had stepped foot here.

She had been a stranger to every single one of them just a few short weeks ago. They might have known her name, but they hadn't known her as a person. But that all changed so quickly as she got to know them. And when they had found out about her award, they had rallied behind her, celebrating her despite the fact that she was planning to leave them. Would anyone in California have done that for her?

She knew the answer immediately. No. They would not have. And somehow, in the weeks that she'd spent in this tiny Christmas town, she'd become a part of them. An unofficial part of the Snowy Pine Ridge community. But it suddenly struck Valerie how much she didn't want it to be unofficial. Not anymore.

She tried to speak again, knowing that everyone was expecting her to come up with some kind of grand speech, but she just couldn't. Valerie could feel the tears building in her eyes, threatening to spill over at any minute.

"I'm so sorry," she muttered, and she wasn't even sure if it was loud enough for anyone to hear. "I need a minute."

She turned, setting her glass of champagne down on a side table as she ran from the room. Valerie took each turn at breakneck speed as she rushed toward the back of the house to the small den that Clark used as a study. She held her hands against her head, pulling air deep into her lungs and exhaling slowly as she paced around the small space.

"Valerie," said a voice from behind her, and she whirled to find Clark standing in the doorway, concern etched into the lines of his face. "Is everything okay?"

She nodded, shook her head, and then nodded again. The tears that had been dancing along the edges of her lash line finally spilled over, and she gave a shaky laugh.

"I don't want to go back," she half sobbed, watching as the confusion on Clark's face turned into realization at her words.

"What do you mean?" he asked hesitantly, taking a careful step toward her.

"I don't want to go back to California," she repeated, her voice sounding more and more confident with every word that she spoke. "I want to stay in Snowy Pine Ridge. I want to be friends with these people, not just acquaintances that I knew for a few weeks during a vacation. Actual, *real* friends. I want to be able to go to Sweet Thing or Baking Fiend every morning, I want to see the Hilton children get older, I want to do things like what Shelley is doing for the kids. I don't want to go."

"What does it mean for your acting, though?"

Clark asked, and Valerie could tell that he was afraid of her answer.

She took a moment, chewing on the inside of her cheek as she took a second to consider. Something Shelley had said to her the night before flickered through her mind, causing an idea to begin to take shape.

"I could travel," she explained. "I could go back and forth. I could fly to wherever the set is whenever I'm working, and then my home base would be here. I could slow down a bit, take roles that I actually loved. Not just because I think they're going to be a hit, but because I'm passionate about the character and the script."

She was getting more and more excited as she spoke, everything seeming to add up and fall into place.

"I could have the best of both worlds!" Valerie exclaimed, suddenly excited at the life she began envisioning. "I could have my career filled with passion and without all the judgment. And I could have..."

Her eyes flicked back to Clark and noting the hesitant look on his face her words died off. She thought he would have been excited at the news, but at the moment he just looked concerned.

"Are you sure this is what you want?" he asked, cocking his head to the side.

Valerie nodded, not needing a moment to think about it, and the worry began to fade from Clark's handsome face. The lines on his forehead eased, relaxing into something else entirely. Joy took over his features as his eyes sparkled and his smile grew wide.

"You know what that means, don't you?" he asked, and Valerie's heart pounded as he wrapped his arms around her waist.

"That I get to keep you too," she murmured, standing up on her tiptoes to brush her lips against his.

"Exactly," he said, and Valerie felt his smile spread even wider before she lost herself in his kiss entirely.

CHAPTER TWENTY-THREE

Two days later, Mindy bustled around Baking Fiend serving customer after customer. It was officially her day of the showcase, and they'd been nonstop all day. She threw a glance over her shoulder toward the employee that was helping her, making sure that she wasn't too swamped at the register as Mindy raced to fulfill the orders.

The night before, Mindy had been worried that she'd made more trifles than she could sell, but now she was terrified that she hadn't made enough. Everyone was buying them, and she could barely keep up with making more in between filling the orders for the customers in the store.

The bell over the door jingled, announcing the arrival of another set of customers, and Mindy glanced up. Her friends were all striding through the door, chatting eagerly as they did so.

"Allison," she said, speaking to the young girl currently waiting behind the counter. "I can take this one from here."

Allison nodded and then walked out to bus some of the tables that had recently been vacated as Shelley, Matthew, Lacy, Derek, Valerie, Clark, Sarah, William, Colette, and Zach all approached the counter.

Valerie was the first in line at the counter, and Mindy immediately broke into a large smile.

"Rumor has it you're going to be staying with us for a while," she surmised, and Valerie gave her an answering grin.

"For as long as you all will have me," she said, prompting Clark to lean in close.

"Which means she'll be here for a very, very long time." He planted a loud kiss on Valerie's cheek, making her groan as Mindy and the others all laughed.

"What is your special for the showcase?" Valerie asked, but then her eyes widened as they darted toward the chalkboard that had the special listed. "A gingerbread trifle? I'll definitely take one of those."

Echoes from the rest of Mindy's friends wanting

to try the showcase menu item sounded, and Mindy rang them all up. She made quick work of grabbing everything for them and then passed the large champagne flutes that contained the desserts over to them.

She waited with bated breath as her friends dipped their spoons into the dessert. People had been raving about the trifle all day, but their opinions were what mattered most. Particularly Sarah, who Mindy quite admired, and a trill of satisfaction rolled through her as Sarah rolled her eyes back in her head, groaning at the taste.

"This is phenomenal," Sarah gushed, dipping her spoon back into the dessert as everyone else murmured their assent.

"Oh, good." Mindy breathed a sigh of relief. "I'm so glad."

They made idle chitchat for a bit, but when another rush of customers came in, Mindy's friends filed out and it was back to running about the space. Hours ticked by, and she was so busy that she hadn't even noticed the familiar form standing at the counter, watching her as Allison did a few things in the back.

Eventually, the man at the counter cleared his throat to grab Mindy's attention, and she whirled to face him. Landon stood just a few feet away. He smiled at Mindy softly as she approached, wiping her hands on her apron before stopping before the register.

"Hey, Landon," she said as she came to a stop before him, giving him a friendly smile. "Thank you for coming in. What can I get for you?"

"I'll take a black coffee and one of the trifles," he answered before fishing in his pocket for his wallet after Mindy gave him a total.

He didn't say anything else as she poured his coffee, grabbed a trifle, and handed it over to him. She waited patiently for him to leave the counter, but he just stood there, eyes roving over her as the corner of his mouth ticked up in a smile.

"Min," he began, his voice taking on a low, intentional tone and Mindy had to fight off a groan. "You look incredible. I was thinking that maybe we could grab dinner or something sometime soon?"

Mindy did sigh then, not wanting to hurt Landon's feelings, but also not wanting to lead him on.

"I don't know if that's a good idea," she began softly, watching as the realization that she was letting him down easy washed over him.

"Oh," he mumbled, nodding his head. "Okay."

Mindy could tell that he was disappointed, and she felt guilty for that, especially as Landon told her he hoped she had a good day and then walked away toward a table. But she knew that they both deserved better than what they'd been giving each other.

She didn't see a future with Landon. In fact, she had never been able to. Mindy could now admit to herself that she'd just been dating him to make her feel a little less alone, and neither of them deserved that. She wanted a love that lit her up from the inside out. The kind of love that made her feel like she was floating.

The image of a familiar face flashed before her mind. A handsome blast from the past that made her heart rate skyrocket, but she quickly stamped the image down. That period of her life was long gone, and it would do no good for her to dwell on it.

She shook her head, clearing her mind of all thoughts except getting through the remainder of the day as Allison came back to the front of the shop and took up her post at the register. Mindy went to the kitchen, beginning to work on another batch of trifles.

She hummed to herself as she worked, allowing the melody of a familiar love song to carry her through her work. And all the while, Mindy was fighting off images of a man she'd once loved. One that got away from her, and one that she would never, ever forget.

* * *

Valerie shifted nervously on the front seat of Clark's truck, wiping her hands along her jeans to help clear them of the sweat that had broken out on them.

"Stop fussing," Clark said with a laugh as he turned the steering wheel to pull into the driveway of their destination. "They're going to love you."

"You might be a little bit biased," Valerie teased, but it didn't stop her stomach from doing flips as the door to Clark's childhood home was pulled open and his mother stepped out onto the porch.

The woman had brown curly hair and vivid green eyes that Valerie could make out at a distance. She was waving at them merrily, and Valerie had to work to steel her nerves.

"It's Christmas," Clark whispered to her the moment before pushing open his door and trotting around the truck so that he could open hers.

It was the first time that Valerie had somewhere to go on Christmas Day since her mother passed away. And the fact that she'd be spending it with

Clark's parents, meeting them for the very first time, had her on the verge of hyperventilating.

The moment that Clark pulled the door open for her, she slid down onto the snow, and it crunched under her boots as they approached the woman on the porch.

"Maureen Mitchell," the woman explained, extending her hand in greeting as the couple approached. "It's a pleasure to meet you. Clark has told me all about you."

Valerie had to fight the urge to blush as she took Maureen's hand and shook it.

"I've heard a lot about you as well," she said warmly.

She had known that his parents knew who she was. Clark had confirmed as much. But he'd also confirmed that they'd promised to not freak out when they met her, and to treat her just like they would any regular old person. Which Valerie appreciated very much.

Maureen opened the door wider, waving them into the house, and Valerie and Clark followed after her. The moment they stepped through the door, Valerie couldn't stop her eyes from darting around the space and taking it all in. Immediately, she noticed the pictures on the walls showing all different stages of the family's lives together. Clark in a t-ball uniform as a child. The three of them on vacation on a beach, beaming like mad at the camera. A ski trip, a graduation. It was all right there, laid out for her along the walls.

They turned a corner and came to a living room that was overflowing with Christmas decorations. A man sat in a fluffy looking recliner in one corner, his gaze glued to the television on the wall.

"Kenneth, we have company," Maureen said, catching the man's attention.

She introduced him to Valerie as Clark's father, and he gave her a kind smile.

"Just watching the parade," he explained, pointing to the TV where a Christmas Day parade filled the screen. "Waiting for the giant glitter Santa Claus balloon. That thing is my favorite."

Everyone chuckled lightly before Maureen turned back to Clark and Valerie.

"I just have a few things to finish up in the kitchen," she said, waving them toward the couch. "Go ahead and sit for a bit. Dinner won't be too much longer."

Valerie tried to offer to help her, but Clark's mother just waved her away affectionately, letting her know that there wasn't much left to do. The smell that filled the house was making Valerie's mouth water as Clark led her to the overstuffed sofa and plopped down.

They began watching the parade with his father, letting Kenneth fill the space with all kinds of fun facts about the different floats, balloons, and sponsors. Valerie loved experiencing this, getting to see a glimpse of what it must have been like for Clark to grow up in this town, what the life that shaped him had been like. And she found herself wanting to learn more and more.

Soon, Maureen came back into the living room and let them all know that dinner was done. When they walked into the dining room, Valerie had to stop herself from gaping. The food looked amazing. A beautiful turkey, mashed potatoes, homemade mac and cheese, rolls, gravy, green beans—the works. Valerie couldn't remember the last time she'd had a meal quite like this.

Clark pulled out her chair for her, motioning for her to sit down before he settled into the chair beside her. As they all filled their plates, Maureen began telling stories about when Clark was younger. The more that Clark's parents talked to her, the more Valerie found that she liked them.

She liked the easy way they interacted with each

other, watching as they shared pointed glances and finished each other's sentences. It was plain as day that the two of them were still madly in love, and Valerie found herself wanting to emulate that one day.

They finished up the meal, which tasted as good as it looked, and then Maureen and Kenneth gave them both soft smiles.

"I know we said we wouldn't," Maureen began.

"But we got you both presents," Kenneth finished, prompting Clark to chuckle and Valerie to smile.

"I should have known you'd break at least one rule," Clark joked.

They were ushered back into the living room as Maureen pulled two presents out from under the tree.

"You truly didn't need to get me anything," Valerie said as she took the package that had been offered to her.

Maureen waved away the sentiment. "It's Christmas and we wanted to."

"Well, thank you, regardless." Valerie began to peel back the wrapping paper at the same time that Clark did.

Both of them ended up unwrapping beautiful,

argyle Christmas sweaters, and Valerie gasped at the sight of hers. It was cream with the print of reindeer along the top, and the material was soft as butter in her hands. She wanted to put it on immediately but figured that might be too much.

"Since it seems like you're going to be staying for a while, we thought you might need something to keep you warm in Snowy Pine Ridge," Kenneth explained, smiling at her.

She smiled at them all, looking between her and Clark's matching sweaters and overwhelmed by the thoughtfulness that had gone into the gifts.

"I plan on staying for a good, long while." Valerie beamed at all of them before meeting Clark's gaze. "So it's absolutely perfect."

And she meant every single word.

CHAPTER TWENTY-FOUR

The day after New Year's, Valerie stood in front of the ice rink, trying to pluck up the courage to walk in. Earlier that day she'd gone to look at an apartment, one that had a lot of promise and that she was contemplating signing a lease on. She'd also called and hired a packing and moving company, arranging the final details of having all of her belongings shipped to her from California.

But now, there was one thing left for her to do, and it was the most terrifying of all.

Valerie marched forward, grabbing hold of the door and giving it a tug. The sound of people laughing as they skated filled the air, as well as the noise and pinging of the arcade farther into the massive building. But Valerie didn't care about any of that. Not as she walked through the space, looking for the man who owned it.

She spotted Shelley at the edge of the rink, watching the kids that were practicing their moves and she caught Shelley's eye. The two women exchanged a quick wave, but Shelley somehow sensed that Valerie wasn't there to see her.

"He's in his office," she called out, nodding her head toward the hallway to Valerie's right. "The door all the way at the end."

She didn't know how Shelley knew that she'd come to see Rudolph, but Valerie was thankful that her friend didn't seem to expect her to explain it. Instead, Shelley just turned her attention back to her students, and allowed Valerie to walk down the hallway toward her destination.

She hesitated outside of the office door, taking a big, deep breath and blowing it out before raising her fist to knock three times on the wooden surface.

"Come in," a gruff voice called from behind the door, and Valerie did as she was told.

"Hi, Rudolph," she said, working her hardest to make sure that her voice remained steady as she spoke.

At the sound of his name, his head shot up in surprise.

"I thought you'd be Shelley," he muttered, blinking up at Valerie in confusion as she offered him a little smile.

"Well, I'm not. I actually wanted to talk to you if you have a moment?"

He nodded, pointing directly toward one of the seats opposite him at the desk, and she pulled one out and sat in it. The metal was cold, even though the fabric of her clothes, and the bite from it made her feel more alert than she had been when she'd first come in.

"I'm moving to Snowy Pine Ridge," Valerie began.

She'd decided on her way to the rink that she was just going to be up front and honest. And, while the statement came out with a little less emotion than she would have liked, she took another deep breath to get control of herself.

"Okay," Rudolph said, slowly nodding his head as he considered her words.

"I just wanted you to know, because..." She gulped past the lump that was forming in her throat. "Well, I'd like to get to know you a little more. If my mother loved you so much, you must be an amazing person. And now that I know about her connection with Snowy Pine

Ridge, how much this place meant to her all makes sense. It was because of you. And I think she'd be happy if we got to know each other a bit. If you're up for it?"

Valerie's heart was beating so hard she was sure that Rudolph would be able to hear it from where he sat. But the man just blinked at her.

At first, she thought he was going to say 'no.' But as she sat there and the seconds ticked on, tears began to form in the corners of his eyes.

"Yeah," he finally said, his voice thick and raspy with emotion. "Yeah, I think I'd like that a lot. And I think Paula would have loved the idea too."

Valerie smiled at him, feeling like a weight had been lifted off her shoulders as they made plans to meet for coffee later that day. And when she stood and finally strode out the door and back out into the rink, a feeling of home washed over her. One that she hadn't felt in quite some time.

* * *

Clark patted the small box in his pocket, reassuring himself that it was still there as he threw the truck in park in the Hiltons' driveway. Valerie was in the front yard, having a snowball fight with Stephanie while Margaret and the other kids watched, laughing, from the large bay window.

"I beat you!" Stephanie yelled as she planted a rather impressively thrown snowball on Valerie's hip.

"Fine, fine." Valerie laughed, and Clark's heart danced at the sound. "You win!"

Stephanie threw her arms over her head, whooping out her enthusiasm but the sound of his truck door closing with a snap startled them both. Their wide eyes whirled toward him, widening a bit before they realized who it was standing before them.

"I'm going to go get a hot chocolate so you can talk to your *boyfriend*," Stephanie teased, giving Valerie a pointed look before sauntering up the porch and disappearing into the house.

Clark and Valerie both laughed, shaking their heads as they watched the seven-year-old run away before they turned to face each other.

"Didn't mean to interrupt all the fun," he said, grinning at her pink cheeks and red tipped nose. "But I have something I couldn't wait to give you."

Valerie's eyes lit up. "A present?"

Clark nodded, reaching into his pocket and pulling out the small jewelry box. Her eyes went wide and glassy at the sight, and Clark couldn't help but laugh at the small bit of panic that lingered in her gaze.

"Calm down," he said with a chuckle. "It isn't a ring box. Just something else I wanted to buy for you."

He opened it up, exposing the delicate silver chain with the silver pendant dangling from it. It had been carved to look like an old-time movie camera, and on the back, he'd had it inscribed with a small bit of text.

Always a star to me. -C

He watched as she picked it up delicately, her beautiful honey-colored eyes wide with wonder as she turned the pendant around in her slender, gloved fingers.

"Clark," she breathed. "It's beautiful."

"Want me to put it on?"

She nodded vigorously, handing the necklace back to him and turning. She held her hair up to give him easy access to secure the jewelry around the delicate column of her throat, and once the clasp was closed, she turned to face him once more.

"How did your agent take the news?" he asked, watching fondly as she ran a finger over the beautiful little pendant.

"Better than I expected," Valerie admitted,

pulling her gaze away from the necklace and back to Clark. "I turned down that role. But she's on the prowl for something else that's a better fit for me. Something that won't require me to be gone so long for filming, and one that has a script that'll knock your socks off."

"That's great," Clark said, nodding. "I know I've said it a thousand times before, but I need to say it again. I support whatever you want to do, even if that means you have to be on the filming site for longer than we'd anticipated."

Valerie threw her arms around his neck, brushing a soft kiss over his lips and grinning.

"You're the best, you know that?"

"I try." Clark shrugged, giving her a grin of his own.

"Thank you for the necklace," she whispered, her voice turning open and honest. "It's beautiful and perfect and so many other words that I can't even think of right now. And it's not just that."

Her gaze turned pensive, and Clark felt a jolt of worry for what was about to come. But when she began to speak again, his fears eased almost immediately.

"And I want to thank you for more than that too," she continued. "You helped me find myself again.

And I can't express how grateful I am that I have you in my life."

He pressed another kiss to her lips, this one softer than the last.

"You don't have to thank me for any of that," he murmured against her lips. "I love doing it. And... I love you."

They broke apart, and Valerie gave a soft gasp as she registered his words. She gazed up at him with emotion filled eyes for a long moment, and he was certain that his heart stopped beating entirely as he waited for her to respond.

Then she let out a soft noise that was halfway between a laugh and a sob. She shook her head, tears shimmering in her eyes even as a radiant smile broke across her face.

"I love you too," she breathed. "So much more than I ever thought possible."

Happiness unfurled within Clark's chest, and he kissed her again. More fiercely this time, letting all of his love pour into her. When they broke apart, they both were a little breathless, and he held her for a while longer, basking in the sweetness of the moment. Then he nodded toward his truck.

"Want to go to Sweet Thing for some pastries and a coffee?"

She glanced at her watch, noting the time, and gave Clark a grin. "Only if you don't mind company. I'm supposed to meet Rudolph there in less than twenty minutes."

"You talked to him then?"

Valerie nodded, telling Clark the full story of how the conversation with the rugged older man had gone. He could tell she was excited about getting to know Rudolph, and he had a feeling that Rudolph felt the same. Who wouldn't want to become better acquainted with this sweet, funny woman?

"I don't mind a bit of company in the slightest," he said, reaching down to intertwine their fingers as he walked toward his truck. "Especially if it's company that I get to share with you."

And with that, they both climbed into the truck, smiling at each other as the sound of Christmas music filled the cab. Clark drove off toward their friend's bakery, his heart nearly bursting with joy. He had everything he needed, right here in the cab of his truck.

For the first time in his life, he felt as if his entire future was unfolding in front of him, allowing him to catch a glimpse of how it would be for the two of them for many, many more evenings to come.

ALSO BY FIONA BAKER

The Marigold Island Series

The Beachside Inn

Beachside Beginnings

Beachside Promises

Beachside Secrets

Beachside Memories

Beachside Weddings

Beachside Holidays

Beachside Treasures

The Sea Breeze Cove Series

The House by the Shore

A Season of Second Chances

A Secret in the Tides

The Promise of Forever

A Haven in the Cove

The Blessing of Tomorrow

A Memory of Moonlight

The Snowy Pine Ridge Series

The Christmas Lodge

Sweet Christmas Wish

Second Chance Christmas

Christmas at the Guest House

A Cozy Christmas Escape

The Christmas Reunion

The Saltwater Sunsets Series

Whale Harbor Dreams

Whale Harbor Sisters

Whale Harbor Reunions

Whale Harbor Horizons

Whale Harbor Vows

Whale Harbor Blooms

Whale Harbor Adventures

Whale Harbor Blessings

For a full list of my books and series, visit my website at www.fionabakerauthor.com!

ABOUT THE AUTHOR

Fiona writes sweet, feel-good contemporary women's fiction and family sagas with a bit of romance.

She hopes her characters will start to feel like old friends as you follow them on their journeys of love, family, friendship, and new beginnings. Her heartwarming storylines and charming small-town beach settings are a particular favorite of readers.

When she's not writing, she loves eating good meals with friends, trying out new recipes, and finding the perfect glass of wine to pair them with. She lives on the East Coast with her husband and their two trouble-making dogs.

Follow her on her website, Facebook, or Bookbub.

Sign up to receive her newsletter, where you'll get free books, exclusive bonus content, and info on her new releases and sales!

Made in the USA
Middletown, DE
25 November 2023